DRE... COME TRUE

JANE CLAYPOOL MINER

SCHOLASTIC BOOK SERVICES

New York Toronto London Auckland Sydney Tokyo

Cover Photo by Owen Brown

No part of this publication may be reproduced in whole or in part, or stored in a retrieval system, or transmitted in any form or by any means, electronic, mechanical, photocopying, recording, or otherwise, without written permission of the publisher. For information regarding permission, write to Scholastic Book Services, 50 West 44 Street, New York, N.Y. 10036.

ISBN 0-590-31566-8

Copyright © 1981 by Jane Claypool Miner. All rights reserved. Published by Scholastic Book Services, a division of Scholastic Magazines, Inc.

12 11 10 9 8 7 6 5 4 3 2 1   2   1 2 3 4 5 6/8

DREAMS CAN
COME TRUE

A Wildfire Book.

WILDFIRE TITLES

Love Comes to Anne by Lucille S. Warner
I'm Christy by Maud Johnson
That's My Girl by Jill Ross Klevin
Beautiful Girl by Elisabeth Ogilvie
Superflirt by Helen Cavanagh
Just Sixteen by Terry Morris
Suzy Who? by Winifred Madison
Dreams Can Come True by
    Jane Claypool Miner

One

The honey and cucumber pack was beginning to feel exactly like a mask of concrete when the phone rang. Ellie grabbed a towel as she ran toward the kitchen. She turned on the hot water faucet and lifted the receiver at the same time. As she spoke, she cradled the phone between her chin and neck, moistened the towel, and began rubbing the hard cream from her face.

"Hi, Lizzie," she said. "I'm in the middle of giving myself a facial."

"We agreed to talk every Friday at this time," Lizzie said.

Ellie thought she heard some hurt in Lizzie's voice and she explained, "I started an hour ago but it took longer than I thought."

"Do you want me to call back?" Lizzie asked.

"Nope. I want to talk to you and wipe this gunk off at the same time. It makes me feel efficient."

Lizzie sighed loudly. "Well, there really isn't so much to tell. August is always dull in Ohio, and it's worse without you. I just don't know how I'm going to get through another year at Middleburg High alone. I mean, here I am in this grubby little town and you're zipping around Hollywood, seeing movie stars, surfing, leading this absolutely wonderful —"

Ellie's laughter stopped the mock complaints. "So far, I've been to Hollywood once for lunch. My mom took me there on the way to the courthouse to do research. It was grim. If there's one place that doesn't live up to the propaganda, it's poor old Hollywood."

"But you do live near the beach," Lizzie reminded her.

"Yes. I can walk to the beach and that's nice. I would have had a miserable summer without that. As it is, I just had a lonely one."

"Is your mom still working night and day?" Lizzie asked sympathetically.

"She still works all the time but she's happier. Ellie, it was the right thing for her to do. Those first three years after my father died, she was so lost. She is really interested in law school. Before, I had the feeling she was working just to keep busy, but things are different now. She laughs more — when I see her."

"Hey, Ellie, I think it's just great that your mother is going to be a famous lawyer. I mean, she may be the Women's Liberation Movement's answer to Perry Mason. I just wish she hadn't moved you to California."

"But my uncle's law firm is in California. She can go in as a junior partner," Ellie reminded her friend.

"Still, it's tough on you to have to start all over again. You were doing so well here."

Ellie bit her lip to keep from telling Lizzie that she didn't agree. After all, what had she really left behind? She missed Lizzie, of course, but she hadn't been exactly a social success during her first two years at Middleburg High. In a way, she was glad she had a second chance here in California. *I won't pick a best friend right away*, she thought. Immediately, she felt guilty. "I just wish you were going to go to Redondo High with me. It would be such fun."

"I don't know," Lizzie sighed again. "It sounds too 'jet setty' for me. Now that you're a glamorous size ten, you'll fit right in, but I'm still lumpy, bookish Lizzie with the heavy eyebrows and thick glasses."

"I lost another pound," Ellie said as she wiped the last of the honey and cucumber paste from her face. "One hundred and ten at last."

"I'm so glad for you! I never thought you'd —"

"But I did and what's more, I'm never going to gain back an ounce. Every time I think about how awful I felt when I was fat, I just shudder. Thirty pounds ago, I hated myself."

"One hundred and forty isn't *that* fat," Lizzie said.

"One hundred and ten is just right," Eleanor countered. "I always dreamed of weighing that."

"Dreams come true. See what I told you, California dreams. You are leading a glamorous life."

Ellie laughed and said, "Sure, sure. The most glamorous part of it is stretching my clothing allowance far enough to get my size ten body covered."

"You don't need clothes in California. Everyone just runs around in bikinis."

"I haven't got a thing. Everything I had in Ohio is either too warm or too big. It's going to be a problem."

"I envy you," Lizzie said. "You've got an excuse to buy all new clothes. I'm still wearing plaid skirts I had in the seventh grade."

"I may have an excuse but I haven't got all that much cash to buy with."

"Make a list. That's what you always do and it works like magic for you." There was admiration in Lizzie's voice now.

Ellie leaned over and opened the refrigerator door. She pulled out a diet soda and struggled to pop the top with one hand as she said, "I guess most people would think my lists were silly, but they really help me get what I want in life. Sometimes, at least."

"I can just see this year's list. It will be nothing but rock stars for boyfriends, designer clothes, a trip to Europe for Christmas. Maybe a movie contract in the spring."

"You're silly. I do miss you." Ellie laughed and talked and drank her soda all at the same time.

"Now that you're such a glamor girl, you might as well go all the way. A name change, a new haircut, a couple of diamonds for your toes, whatever it takes to fit the new image."

"Actually, I *am* changing my name from Eleanor to Ellynne." She pronounced it to rhyme with "again."

"See what I mean!" Lizzie teased triumphantly. "No more Ellie for the glamor girl. Now she wants a name fit for stardom. Next thing you know, she'll be dating the football hero and trying out for cheerleader."

Ellie blushed. Lizzie was fun but sometimes her humor cut too close to the bone. How did she know that she had spent a lot of time on the beach this summer dreaming of exactly that? It was a daydream, of course, but why did Lizzie imply it was ridiculous? Why shouldn't she date a football hero and be a cheerleader? Other girls did. She interrupted Lizzie and said, "It's eleven-twenty in Ohio. Even at cheap rates, we're going to be broke."

"You're right," Lizzie agreed. "We've got to be thrifty. You need your money for glad rags."

"Glad rags! Where do you get words like that?"

"Comes from reading old romances. Softens the brains and teaches you a lot of outdated slang. By the way, I think I've got a part-time job in the library. Mrs. Barnes says she can hire me on Saturdays to shelve books."

"That's wonderful news! Why didn't you tell me right away?"

"Oh, it didn't seem so important." Lizzie's voice seemed unsure of herself and a bit shy now.

They talked of Lizzie's new job until midnight, in Ohio, and then said good-bye. Ellie felt a sense of loss as she hung the phone up. She missed Lizzie a lot, and these weekly conversations had really kept her from feeling too sorry for herself this summer. She and her mother had been in Redondo Beach for six weeks now and Eleanor didn't know a soul. She saw kids from a distance at the beach but no one spoke. It was frightening to move from a small, mid-Western town to a big, confusing place like Redondo Beach, California. She was glad that Lizzie was still her friend and that they could keep in touch.

As she painted her toenails and shampooed her hair, Ellie reviewed the conversation she'd just had. It was funny how close Lizzie had come to guessing her secret dreams. But then, she and Lizzie had been best friends since the seventh grade.

And she was right about my lists, Ellie thought. *They do help me.* She stepped out of the tub, dried briskly, and wrapped herself up in her blue terry bathrobe. Critically, she looked at herself in the mirror. As far as she could see, the honey and cucumber mask hadn't worked any miracles. Still, she couldn't complain. Now that she was thinner, her cheekbones made her wide, green eyes seem almost slanted, and she knew her straight nose and wide mouth gave her an interesting look. She wasn't so bad, though it was true that her mouse-brown hair was too thin and straight, and she did wish her eyebrows weren't so wide.

Ellie went into her bedroom, locked the door, though the house was empty, took out her secret notebook, and started making a list.

Ever since she was a youngster of ten, Ellie had been keeping secret notebooks. They weren't exactly diaries, but they were more than the lists that Lizzie called them. In her own mind, Ellie thought of her notebooks as dreambooks.

It was a brand-new notebook that Ellie opened this night. She looked at the smooth, white page and wrote her new name, Ellynne Aleese, with a large, broad stroke of her felt-tip pen.

On the next page, she wrote the words, A New Image. Underneath that, she wrote a list: 1) new name, 2) new clothes, 3) new attitudes, 4) new friends, 5) new interests.

She worked quite a while on the next section, which she labeled, New Clothes For The New Image.

New Clothes took three pages. First, she wrote down everything she had that she wanted to keep. There wasn't much. Most of it would have to go to the Goodwill. Next, she wrote down everything that she could imagine she would like to have. That list was long and extravagant. On the third page, Ellynne listed the items that seemed most essential to her needs and new image. Even trying to be practical, Ellynne realized that her list was about three times longer than the three hundred dollars she had to spend. Three hundred dollars seemed like a lot of money until you divided it into actual purchases. Ellynne hesitated a long time before she crossed out the wonderful corduroy blazer she'd seen for sixty-three dollars at the Shopping Plaza. It was a great blazer, but she couldn't afford to spend one-fifth of her clothing budget on it.

Soon, Ellynne had a firm list for clothes. She also had some definite ideas about how she was going to go about attracting the sort of friends she really wanted to have at Redondo High when she got there next week. At the top of that list was the word, CAUTION. She was sure that the worst thing she could do was make friends too quickly. She wanted to take her time, look the situation over, and select a group of friends who were the sort that would be fun to be with.

The list for New Attitudes was shorter. In fact, there were only five lines on the list. They were:

1. Act interested in everything.
2. Be friendly but careful.
3. Be cheerful and laugh more.
4. Don't say dumb things about your-self.
5. Expect to be popular.

Perhaps it was sleepiness that led her to write an imaginary scene instead of a list on the pages set aside for New Interests.

She started out by writing the title, New Interests, across the top of the paper, but then she slipped into a daydream about the first day of school. She was walking down the hall and a lot of people turned around and looked at her. They were all very friendly and several came up to her and started talking.

One of the boys who introduced himself was tall, good-looking, and had a wonderful smile. She couldn't quite imagine what he looked like beyond that, but she did know he was very attractive. Idly, Ellynne named him Derek and she began to write an imaginary conversation in her secret notebook.

Derek: Say, you're that mysterious new girl, aren't you?

Me: I'm new. My name is Ellynne Aleese.

Derek: (*smiling*) Ellynne Aleese. Suits you. Yes, you look like a girl who would be called Ellynne. Beautiful. No wonder . . .

Me: No wonder what?

Derek: No wonder everyone is talking about you. I'm captain of the football team here and we need a new cheerleader. Ever do any cheerleading?

Me: Not really. Of course, I've watched it.

Derek: You could do it, Ellynne. You've got grace and beauty. You've got what it takes. Would you consider?

Scene shifts. It is the first half-time of the first football game of the season. The team is losing. Ellynne Aleese steps out in front of the crowd. She is wearing a pink and red plaid skirt and a pink sweater. Her pompoms are made with silk ribbons. Her cheers are so great that the stands shake and the crowd roars. She saves the game. Scene shifts to the Homecoming Dance. Ellynne, who is Homecoming Queen, is dancing with Derek.

Derek: My darling, you are so beautiful tonight.

Me: And you are the most wonderful man in the world.

Guiltily, Ellynne stared at the little play she'd written in her secret notebook. She would feel horrible if anyone ever read it.

She started to tear the sheets out and then she stopped. What was it that Lizzie had said? *"Your lists work like magic for you."*

Well, if lists worked like magic, maybe this play could work too. It wouldn't hurt to leave it there. After all, it was a daydream, but people needed dreams to point them where they were headed.

She left the play where it was and put the secret notebook back inside the locked drawer of her desk. Her mother wasn't a snoop, but Ellynne liked having a private book in a private compartment in her private room.

She turned off her light and went to sleep, positively cheered at the prospect of her new name. It was all part of a wonderful new life she was going to have here in Southern California. She was almost looking forward to her first day of school, especially since she was clear what she wanted for her new image.

Two

Ellynne knew her mother would have preferred not to be involved in shopping for school clothes at all. Still, she'd gone with Ellynne and watched patiently as Ellynne tried on six yellow cardigan sweaters before she found the perfect one.

At lunch, her mother teased. "You knew exactly what you were going to buy before you even came."

"Thanks for coming anyway," Ellynne said. "It's no fun to shop alone."

Even with company, shopping for school clothes wasn't much fun this year. Everything was so expensive and her mother kept suggesting things that just weren't possible at all.

By two o'clock, they were both tired and her mother wanted to go home, but Ellynne said, "Not until I get my jeans."

Her mother sighed, rolled her eyes heavenward, and said, "Come on, Ellie. Jeans are jeans. You can pick them up anywhere."

"Jeans are not jeans and don't call me Ellie. My name is Ellynne."

"Your name is Eleanor Louise Aleese and that's that," Judith Aleese retorted grimly.

They said no more until Ellynne stopped at the designer jeans rack and pulled out a pair of blue jeans with small, diagonal pockets and a leather tab on the back. The tab had the name, Claire Johnson, stamped in gold.

Her mother said, "They're nice. How much are they?"

"Thirty-four dollars."

"You're kidding?"

Ellynne didn't bother to reply but went into the dressing room. They looked wonderful and she slid out of them quickly. Coming out of the dressing room, her mother asked, "You're not really going to spend thirty-four dollars for a pair of blue jeans?"

Ellynne nodded and headed toward the cashier's counter.

Her mother raised her voice, "Eleanor Louise, that is the most ridiculous thing I've ever seen. You spent all morning pinching pennies, weighing one gray flannel skirt against another as though they were made of gold. Now you buy the first pair of blue jeans you try on and they cost a fortune — an absolute fortune."

A couple of shoppers turned to look at her mother. Ellynne winced as she said as calmly as she could, "It's *my* clothing money."

"You drag me out with you and then you don't listen to a word I say! I could be home studying!" Judith Aleese huffed.

"You don't care about anything but that dumb old law school," Ellynne retorted. She turned from her mother and gave the money to the cashier, who stuffed the expensive pants into a sack, stapled the receipt on the outside, and called, "Next."

Ellynne followed her mother out to the car and they drove home in silence. At the door, her mother said, "I know I was cross in the store. You're free to spend your clothing money as you wish. You're older and capable of making your own decisions. You can wear a barrel to school if they'll let you in, for all I care."

"I'm sorry I dragged you along." Ellynne apologized immediately.

It felt good to be on pleasant terms with her mother again, but she was pretty discouraged about her purchases. She'd found most of the things on her list, but somehow, the clothes she'd chosen seemed almost too well-planned. Ellynne hung up the new gray skirt, smoothed out the navy pleated one and folded her yellow, pink, and white sweaters carefully.

It would have been nice to have one thing that was more of a surprise. *Not* the pink and orange striped tee shirt that her mother tried to talk her into, but something unusual. She held her new pink sweater up and looked in the mirror. It was very pretty. Had she expected too much? Somehow, she'd thought that the clothes she would be able to find in size ten would be a whole lot better than the size fourteens she used to wear.

Ellynne shook her head to clear her thoughts, put her sweaters in her drawer, and pulled on her cut-off jeans and an old tee shirt. She would walk along the beach before supper, and this evening she'd do her nails, wash her hair, and get ready for the first visit to her new school. Tomorrow was Tuesday and she would be registering, even though school would not start until Wednesday.

The next morning her mother looked up from her newspaper with an amused interest in Ellynne's appearance. She said, "You look very nice but don't you think it's a bit warm for that sweater?"

Ellynne shook her head, poured herself some skim milk, and ate a slice of cheese on wheat bread. She said, "Mother, I want you to promise me you won't call me Ellie in front of any of the kids."

Her mother sighed and said, "Ellie, I don't know what's the matter with you. You've become so frivolous and artificial. You're a nice girl just the way you are. You don't need fancy names and designer jeans. You need an education."

"I want to be popular, Mother. Is that so hard for you to understand? Believe me, it's important."

She shook her head. "Ellie, you will be popular. You're a nice, bright, wholesome girl with plenty to offer. You have always had lots of friends and this school will be bigger and better. You'll see."

In the car, her mother tried to make small talk. "Why didn't you wear those fancy blue jeans today? Seems as though they'd be an auspicious beginning."

Ellynne didn't answer. Her heart was beating loudly and she was feeling just awful. It was all very well for her mother to say that Redondo High was going to be bigger and better, but she wasn't so sure. In her old school, she'd just been an ordinary kid and this one was three times larger. She'd be lucky if anyone spoke to her before Christmas.

The sun was beating down even though it was only nine in the morning. Ellynne was already sorry she'd worn her old sweater and new pleated skirt. She should have known it would be hot. September was one of the hottest months in California, and she should have planned better.

They walked up the wide marble steps to the main entrance of Redondo High School in silence. Ellynne wished she didn't have to make her first appearance at school with her mother, but it was a legal necessity. Besides, there probably wouldn't be any other kids around.

But Ellynne was wrong about that. A whole group of girls stood laughing and talking just inside the main entrance of the school. They all wore green armbands and white blouses. Ellynne saw that they had piled heavy, green, school sweaters in one chair. These were obviously important girls who belonged to some special club. Ellynne gulped and tried to walk past them.

A tall, slim, exotically beautiful black girl walked up to them. She said, "Hi, I'll show you where the office is."

The girl walked a half-step ahead of them and Ellynne had to smile when her mother whispered, "She's got your blue jeans on."

Ellynne had known all along that they were the right pants to buy. She felt good about that and when they stepped inside the office she turned to their guide and said, "Thanks."

"I'll wait. I'm going to show you around." The girl tilted her head slightly and her gold hoop earrings glittered in the sunlight pouring through the office window. She seemed to be looking Ellynne over carefully.

Ellynne's attention was divided between wondering what the young woman was thinking about her and worrying about what her mother was going to say to the school secretary.

Her guide asked, "You're from New England?"

Ellynne shook her head and said, "Ohio." At that moment, she had to turn to the desk because she'd just heard the clerk ask for her name. She had to stop her mother . . .

But her mother said clearly and firmly, "Ellynne Aleese. You may notice it is Eleanor on her old records but we want that changed. We never call Ellynne anything but Ellynne."

Good old Mom. Ellynne sighed deeply and turned back to her guide. The girl said, "Ellynne. What a pretty name. My name is Wilhelmina Evans, but of course all they ever call me is Willie. Willie Evans, that's me." She held out her hand for Ellynne to shake.

Ellynne was surprised and slightly startled by this girl's direct manner. Funny how someone could look so glamorous and be so straightforward.

Willie was talking faster now. "I would have sworn you were from New England. You've got that genteel thing that they all seem to have." She laughed aloud. "Not that I've known that many New Englanders, but I'm going to study fashion in college and I read all the magazines."

The secretary looked up from the forms and said sharply, "Willie, you're here to be helpful, not tell your life story."

Willie didn't seem the least bit embarrassed. She just grinned at Ellynne and stuck her thumbs in the small, diagonal pockets of her Claire Johnson jeans as she stepped into a wider stance and assumed a model's pose. She leaned against the wall looking absolutely relaxed and sophisticated at the same time. Ellynne envied Willie's casual assurance.

It didn't take long for Ellynne to be enrolled, since they'd had the foresight to have all her records mailed last June. The school was expecting her and everything was completed quickly. Her mother looked at her watch and said cheerfully, "Great. I've got time to drive to the law library before noon."

Willie moved toward them and said, "You get the Grand Tour now. I'm going to show you all around the place."

Judith Aleese looked at her daughter for a moment. Ellynne stood silently, hoping her mother could find the time to take the tour with her. In spite of Willie's apparent friendliness, Ellynne felt stiff and uncomfortable. She couldn't help thinking that Willie Evans was just being friendly because she was supposed to and that made Ellynne feel shy.

Her mother said, "Thank you. We'd like that."

For the second time today, Ellynne silently thanked her mother for being such a good sport.

Willie took them up the stairs and down the halls and through the library and behind the stage. All the time they walked, Willie talked non-stop about school activities, her own future plans, and how happy Ellynne was going to be at Redondo High School.

By the time they got to the cafeteria, Ellynne knew that Willie's father was a psychiatrist, that she had two brothers and one sister, and that she was in the Women's Service Club, on the cheerleading team, and sometimes a part-time model.

The more Willie talked, the more insignificant Ellynne felt. She could barely answer when Willie tossed out questions in the middle of her cheerful monologue. When Willie asked, "What are your hobbies, Ellynne?"

"None, I guess," Ellynne answered shyly.

"Ellie!" her mother scolded. "You do so many things! You've got your writing and your painting and your record collection."

If Willie noticed that her mother called her Ellie, she ignored it. Willie Evans seemed to be the sort of girl who slid over difficulties with the grace of a figure skater. She was pointing out the language laboratory with all its fancy equipment now, and she seemed to find that just as interesting as any other part of her assignment.

As they climbed up the stairs to the main entrance, Willie asked, "Do you ever model?"

"No." It was a whisper. Was this girl making fun of her?

"I thought you might. You've got a perfect figure. Size seven?"

"Ten."

Willie shook her head in mock dismay. "Wrong on two counts. Not a New Englander and not a size seven. Well, I'm sure I'm right about this guess. I guess we're going to be good friends, Ellynne Aleese."

Willie shook hands with Judith and Ellynne and then stood on the step watching them walk down to their car. At one point, Judith Aleese turned and said to Ellynne, "She's waving. Wave back."

Ellynne felt absolutely stifling in the navy sweater. She wanted to yell at her mother, but she knew that would be unfair. She turned and waved to Willie and ducked into the car.

Once inside, her mother said cheerfully, "Well, talk about luck! You've already met the nicest girl you could. She'd be a good friend, no matter what, but she also happens to be very popular. Anyone could see that."

"She was just being nice," Ellynne answered gloomily.

"That's what I like to see," her mother teased lightly. "Positive thinking in action. Expect the best and what do you get?"

"The best," Ellynne answered dully. She'd heard this lecture before and she was trying, she was really trying. Still, it was clear to see that a girl who looked like Willie Evans and was as self-confident and happy as she obviously was, wasn't going to need her.

"That's right," her mother agreed. "And from what I saw, Willie Evans looked like one of the best, all right."

Three

On the morning of the first day of school, Ellynne was up at six, trying to calm the butterflies in her stomach as she dressed. She didn't have to worry about what to wear because she'd planned that very carefully the night before.

She pulled on her new designer jeans, her best white cotton shirt, and tied a pink scarf around her neck. She wore last spring's espadrilles and a thin leather pink belt that she'd salvaged from one of her mother's old dresses. She would carry the new pink cardigan, perhaps tossing it casually around her shoulders, if the day was a cool one.

Ellynne stared at herself in the mirror for a long time. Even though she'd been slim for a while, she couldn't get used to the idea. She'd lost thirty pounds over a period of five months, on a slow and sensible diet, and the change had been gradual. She knew that the tall, slim girl in the skin-tight jeans was the same old Ellie, Eleanor, Ellynne Aleese, but it was hard to believe.

Will I always feel fat? Ellynne wondered. She'd read that some people who lost weight never got used to it, and she'd also read that most people regained their lost weight very quickly. Ellynne had determined that she would be the exception. Simple meals were a small price for looking like this, she decided.

Even though she was satisfied with her appearance, Ellynne could not quell the nervous feeling as she ate her breakfast, looked over the morning headlines, and washed her dishes. Glancing at her watch, she saw it was only seven-fifteen and even if she walked slowly, it was too early to start for school.

Idly, Ellynne went back into her room, opened her desk, and took out her secret notebook. She glanced over her lists and plans that she'd been working on the last few weeks. *If only life would follow scripts,* Ellynne sighed.

It was all there for her to see — her hopes and dreams of popularity, of new friends, of new adventures. She closed her eyes and resolved that no matter what, she would expect the best today. And if she didn't get the best immediately, well, she'd keep on working at it.

She closed her notebook, put it back in her desk, picked up her pink sweater, and started for the door. As she passed her mother's room, Judith Aleese called out, "See you for lunch?"

"School's out at eleven-thirty today. I'll be home." In her secret plans, she had listed a lunch invitation from Willie Evans, but she knew that was only a dream. Why would Willie want to invite her to lunch? She'd be lucky if the girl spoke to her. It would be a miracle if Willie remembered her name.

The sun wasn't bright this morning, and Ellynne was grateful for the pink sweater that she was wearing as she walked to school. Redondo Beach was a nice place to live, but there was a lot of fog and the mist off the ocean made it damp and chilly. Ellynne knew the dampness would burn off as soon as the fog lifted, but right now she was shivering and glad to get inside the building.

Ellynne found her homeroom with no difficulty and slipped quietly into her seat. She looked around the room at the other students, all of whom seemed to know each other. There was a lot of laughing, gossip, and swapping of stories. Ellynne wondered if she were the only new person in the room.

On the way out of homeroom, a boy came up to her and said, "You're new here, aren't you?"

Ellynne smiled and answered, "Yes, I am. I'm Ellynne Aleese." She was relieved to hear that her voice sounded relaxed and cheerful.

"Bruce Davidson," he replied. "Know where you go next?"

Ellynne held out her program card and said, "English 211. That's the second floor?"

"I'll show you the way," Bruce offered.

He was tall and broad-shouldered, with straight blonde hair and horn-rimmed glasses. He seemed shy and friendly at the same time.

"I wanted to make sure to get to know you fast," Bruce said. "You'll probably be surrounded by guys by noon."

Ellynne blushed. It was like one of her scripts! She thanked Bruce politely for showing her to her English class and ducked inside the door before he could say anything else. Although it was fun to have someone show such obvious interest in her, she wanted to be very careful not to form any "wrong" friendships the first weeks.

Ellynne knew enough about high school to know that the worst thing you could do was get branded as part of the wrong crowd. If Bruce Davidson turned out to be a weirdo it would be a disaster to have him around.

Be friendly but cautious, her planbook had said, and she intended to follow that resolution. Still, it was wonderful to have someone pay attention to her so quickly, and he had seemed nice enough.

Homeroom, English, then math and homeroom again. The first day was only a half-day and she wouldn't even get to know all of her classes. She looked around the classrooms hopefully, thinking that there was a possibility that Willie would be in one of them. After all, she knew that they were both college prep students and juniors. It could happen.

But Willie wasn't in either class and she didn't meet her in the halls. Another boy offered to walk her to her math class. Ellynne was delighted and amused by the attention she was getting. Either the students at Redondo High School were exceptionally friendly or she was getting exceptional attention.

This one's name was Arnold and he told her right away that he was on the football team. "That's wonderful," Ellynne replied.

"You interested in football?" he asked hopefully.

"I love football," Ellynne said breathlessly. In her mind she could see rule number one in New Attitudes. Be enthusiastic about everything.

"Maybe we'll be seeing a lot of each other then," Arnold said.

"That would be nice," Ellynne answered. "Thanks for walking me to class."

"I'll pick you up after class."

"Oh, that's not necessary," Ellynne assured him. "I can find my way back to homeroom."

"Sure?"

"Sure," Ellynne said firmly. Though Arnold also seemed nice, she just didn't want the feeling that she was being rushed by anyone.

Ellynne left her homeroom and started out the main entrance of the school toward her home at eleven-thirty. It had been a day which far exceeded her expectations. Everything had gone so smoothly and well, she was really grateful, though it would have been nice to run into Willie.

She was halfway down the stairs before she heard someone calling to her. For a minute, she didn't turn around. Then she decided that there couldn't be any mistake. It was definitely her name that was being called, "Ellynne. Ellynne Aleese."

She turned, and there was Willie Evans standing at the top of the stairs, waving frantically. Ellynne waved back and took a step away. Willie motioned for her to climb the stairs again, shouting, "Come back up."

Ellynne climbed up to the top of the stairs and Willie said, "I thought I was going to miss you. I just got to school about thirty minutes ago. Twisted my ankle." She raised her blue-jeans pants leg and showed Ellynne the slim brown ankle, which was wrapped in an Ace bandage.

"How did you do that?"

Willie made a face. "You'd think it would be an exciting story, but it's just a dumb one. My cat sleeps with me, and when the alarm rang we jumped out of bed at the same time, but I jumped on her. She's all right, of course, but I'm an invalid."

"That's too bad."

"Sure is. Especially since I'm supposed to lead the cheers at Friday's game. Well, anyway, I'm sorry I can't invite you to have lunch at my house. I'd planned to ask you and some of the other kids, but now I have to go home and soak my foot. Dumb, dumb, dumb."

Ellynne was so delighted to discover that Willie had intended to invite her to lunch, she didn't even feel disappointed. She said, "Some other time. And thanks."

Willie nodded briefly and said, "Let's see your schedule. Maybe we have the same classes."

Though Ellynne had received her schedule when she registered two days ago, the returning students at Redondo High found out who their teachers were in homeroom that morning.

Ellynne held out her schedule card and Willie checked it against her own, hopping and then wincing with pain as she said, "Great! We've got gym and social together."

"That's great," Ellynne agreed.

"I'm sorry about today," Willie repeated. "But tomorrow, we'll get together at lunch. I eat at the same table every day, with the same kids. You can eat with us."

"Thanks," Ellynne said gratefully. She had worried a lot about whom she would eat with those first few days, until she made some permanent friends. Now, it seemed that even that problem was solved.

"How did you like Redondo High?" Willie asked.

Ellynne laughed out loud at the question. "Like? I *love* Redondo High!"

Willie smiled broadly and nodded in approval. "Good girl. With an attitude like that, you won't have a bit of trouble."

Four

For the first full day of school, Ellynne chose her gray skirt and a yellow striped shirt she'd bought when she first started losing weight. The blouse was a size thirteen and too big but she pulled it in with a wide leather belt. Her new yellow sweater would look good across her shoulders but it would probably be too warm to wear.

Her mother, who was going to law school in the late afternoons and evenings, had left her a note. Ellynne opened the envelope and read eagerly, "Ellie, I'm so glad you liked school. Here's a small present to celebrate your beautiful beginnings. I'm proud of you." There was twenty dollars in the envelope and Ellynne drew in her breath in surprise.

Judith Aleese had very definite opinions about how to handle money, and Ellynne had been on a moderate allowance ever since her father died. It wasn't like her mother to make a gift of money, but this twenty was a welcome change in habit.

Ellynne tucked the money into her money drawer in her desk and rinsed her dishes before she went to school. Though she was still nervous, she was almost looking forward to this day. She would be eating lunch with Willie and maybe one of the boys who'd walked her to class yesterday would speak to her again today. *It might not be too bad,* she thought. Then she whispered, "Expect the best, expect the best, expect the best."

The morning classes seemed terribly long because each teacher spent all period talking in general terms about the content of the course. Though they all threatened a great deal of work, no one actually gave any, and by fourth period Ellynne was shifting in her seat, doodling in her notebook, and even making a new list.

She was going to use that twenty to get a pair of cord levis in a color, she decided. Most of the girls at Redondo High were wearing pants, and Ellynne didn't want to be branded as conservative or old-fashioned. In Ohio, the girls had been wearing skirts more and more, but apparently Californians weren't as moved by the fashion magazines as were mid-Westerners. She would have to talk to Willie about that.

". . . What do you think about that, Miss Aleese?" the science teacher asked.

Ellynne blushed as she heard her name

called. She stammered, "I wasn't listening, I'm sorry."

The science teacher nodded briefly, looking at her as though he'd pegged her as a permanently poor student, and went on to another person on his seating chart. "Miss Merriweather, what do you think?"

Ellynne turned slightly and saw a darling-looking girl with short, curly brown hair, a turned-up nose, and pink cheeks. Merri Merriweather seemed to bubble enthusiasm as she replied, "It just seems to me it would be really wrong, Mr. Morales, no matter what the scientists say I mean, I wouldn't want to go out on a date with some guy, get interested in him, maybe even be thinking of marrying him, and then discover he was a *clone*!"

The class laughed loudly at Merri's reply and the science teacher frowned crossly. "I can see that I'm beset with a bevy of bird-brains."

Merri's little laugh tinkled across the class. She seemed quite pleased with the attention and didn't seem the least bit concerned about being called a birdbrain. Ellynne blushed again and straightened up in her seat. She was a good student ordinarily and she didn't like it at all.

Though she raised her hand twice, Mr. Morales didn't call on her again, and Ellynne left the class feeling quite defeated by the first day's events. It was clear that she'd made a poor impression on her science teacher and that might take weeks to erase. Teachers were tough when they made up their minds about you.

Perhaps it was the embarrassing experience in science, perhaps she would have been nervous anyway, but Ellynne dawdled as she went to her locker for her lunch, then entered the cafeteria hesitantly. She stood at the edge of the room, which seemed as large as a football field, and looked for Willie Evans. Nowhere did she see her. In fact, she was so scared that she couldn't really see much.

She had just about decided to skip lunch and go to the library, when she heard Willie calling her name. Following the direction of the call, Ellynne spotted Willie who was standing up, waving frantically and motioning for her. Feeling very shy, Ellynne walked over to a table that was set in the very corner of the cafeteria, beside the sliding glass doors that opened onto the patio.

When she got to the table, Willie apologized, "I would have been waiting for you at the doorway but this darn ankle is still sore."

"I'm glad I found you," Ellynne said. She looked with alarm at the table of kids she was supposed to join. They didn't look too friendly as she squeezed in beside Willie and another girl. Willie introduced her to everyone in hearing distance and Ellynne nodded to each one separately.

Right then, Merri Merriweather came up to the table, carrying a tray, and said, "Hi, Willie. Scoot over, will you. There's not much room."

Willie said, "Merri, this is Ellynne Aleese from Ohio," as Merri pushed herself into a place between Willie and the wall.

Merri nodded and said, "Saw you in science." Merri immediately began talking to the girl across from her and Ellynne felt vaguely snubbed though she wasn't sure exactly why. She opened her lunch and took out the food she'd prepared for herself. She would have liked to buy milk but she couldn't bear to get up from the table and walk across that huge cafeteria. Most of the kids seemed to be ignoring her, but she could see them sneaking glances when she wasn't supposed to be looking. She knew they were waiting to see if she would fit in before they became too friendly. Well, she couldn't blame them for that, that was the way things were.

It was clear that this table was full of some of the most popular kids in the school. Funny how quickly you could tell a thing like that, just by the way others who walked by looked at them. One girl stopped and stood talking to Merri, obviously hoping for an invitation to sit down. A couple glanced enviously at

Ellynne and the question behind the glance was, "How do you rate?"

Ellynne cracked her egg and began peeling it. Merri looked up from her plate of spaghetti and said, "Ugh! I hate hard-boiled eggs." She looked at the half sandwich on whole wheat bread and the carrot sticks and apple that Ellynne had in front of her and asked, "Do you always eat icky food like that or are you on a diet?"

Ellynne decided right then that she didn't want Merri to know she had ever been fat. She said, "I like eggs."

"Ugh!" Merri said again. "But carrot sticks! You have to be on a diet."

Willie looked up sharply and said, "Merri, Ellynne has a perfect figure. That's because she eats right. Look at the calories on your plate."

Merri laughed. "I'll work them off practicing cheers."

"How's it going?" the girl beside Merri asked.

Merri answered, "O.K. I don't suppose I'll have any trouble but I want to make sure."

"Are you a cheerleader too?" Ellynne asked. She wanted to be friendly and she was grateful that the talk was off her lunch.

Merri shook her head and answered, "Willie's the only junior who is on the cheerleading team. I'm working on next year."

"Tryouts are in the spring," Willie said

dryly. Ellynne had the impression that Willie wasn't one hundred percent crazy about Merri Merriweather.

But even if Willie wasn't absolutely sold on Merri, it was clear that everyone else thought she was special. People called from down at the other end of the table to ask her questions. A couple of boys stopped to talk with her. Ellynne ate her lunch and watched carefully.

Willie Evans and Merri Merriweather were like two princesses being courted by the commoners. People passed by the table, obviously trying to become as friendly as they dared. By the time she'd eaten the last carrot stick, Ellynne realized that she'd been very, very lucky to meet Willie on registration day. It might have taken weeks to get to know her. In fact, she might never have had the chance.

As though she read her mind, Merri said out loud, "You were lucky to get Willie as your guide. I forgot my new kid. We were supposed to eat lunch with them the first day." Merri looked around vaguely, as though she'd just remembered. Then she said, "Of course, there wouldn't have been room for her. This table is so crowded."

Ellynne felt awful. She wondered if Merri was deliberately being mean to her. Well, she was determined to make the best of it. Ellynne said, "Yes, I was lucky. And it was nice to meet you all." There, even if she never sat at this table again, she'd been polite.

Willie spoke quietly but with the determination of a hero in a Western movie who was carrying six-shooters. "Ellynne will be eating here every day. She's my friend. I like a girl with class."

Ellynne smiled gratefully at Willie. There was no question about who was Chief Princess. Willie obviously did and said what she wanted, to Merri and anyone else. Willie was a lot of wonderful things and the most wonderful of all seemed to be that she was an independent spirit.

Merri was nicer to Ellynne after that and seemed to accept without a struggle the notion that she was going to be a permanent friend of Willie's. They talked about cheers for most of the rest of the lunch period.

Ellynne relaxed and enjoyed the sense of belonging that was coming over her as she sat beside her new friend. She knew it wasn't going to be this easy forever, but she was grateful for the smooth beginning.

About the time she was totally relaxed, she looked up and saw the best-looking boy she'd ever seen come toward them. He was tall and broad-shouldered with the easy manner and walk of an athelete. She wasn't sure exactly what it was about him that was so special, but she did know that he was very, very special.

She stared at him as he came over to their table. He had clear blue eyes and his hair was darker than she'd thought from a distance. In fact, it seemed to have a few reddish glints to it and it curled around his ears. He was so handsome that Ellynne actually drew in her breath, as he got nearer.

When he got to the table, Merri said, "I don't know where you're going to sit. It's so crowded."

Ellynne blushed a deep red. She was sure Merri wanted her to leave so this handsome fellow could sit down.

"I don't want to sit," he replied quickly. "I just wanted to ask you about tonight."

"Seven-thirty." Merri replied.

Ellynne looked down at the apple in front of her. Would anyone introduce her to this young man? Her heart was beating wildly and her hands felt clammy. Funny, she'd never had a reaction like this to any fellow before. But this was what it must be like to fall in love at first sight.

Willie said, "Kip, this is Ellynne Aleese from Ohio."

Ellynne looked up and smiled shyly. "Hello," was all she could manage to say.

She shouldn't have bothered. Kip Russell didn't even look at her. His deep blue eyes skipped lightly over her without seeing and he said, "See you at seven-thirty," to Merri. Then he turned and left.

Ellynne wanted to cry. Why couldn't things be the way they were in books? She had met the most important man in her life and he hadn't even looked at her. He wouldn't even recognize her in the halls. Wryly, she thought of her silly little dreams she'd written in her secret notebook.

She watched Kip Russell walk away and a sadness came over her. She didn't know much about him yet but she felt that he was important to her. Everything about him seemed perfect. He moved swiftly, quietly through the lunch crowd and out of the cafeteria.

"I hope I didn't have his seat," Ellynne said to no one in particular.

Merri laughed. "Kip thinks he's going to be a famous scientist. He spends his lunch hours in the lab helping Mr. Morales." She sighed heavily. "It's a problem dating a boy like Kip. He's so ambitious that he isn't much fun."

"But it's wonderful that he's going to make something of his life." Ellynne defended Kip Russell quickly.

Merri looked at her with an amused, superior air. "Count on Kip to knock them dead every time."

Ellynne blushed and bit into the apple. Willie changed the subject and nothing else was said about Kip Russell except when they talked of the football team's chances this year, Ellynne discovered that Kip was captain of the team. *It figures*, she told herself.

Talk about impossible dreams! Here she'd fallen for the football captain who also happened to date one of the most popular girls in the school. *Nothing like aiming for the moon,* she teased herself, but she didn't really think it was funny.

Five

Ellynne didn't see Kip Russell for the next two days. She learned most of the names of the people who sat at the lunch table with Willie, and they spoke to her when she passed them in the halls. Ellynne knew she was lucky to have made friends so quickly, and she was deeply grateful to Willie.

Willie really was as wonderful as she'd seemed that first day. She laughed when Ellynne tried to thank her for her help. "I'm just so glad to meet someone with class!" Willie replied, and then she tossed her head and smiled broadly.

Ellynne wasn't exactly sure what Willie meant when she said she had *class*, but she was sure it was good and she was sure that Willie was a person who stuck to the decisions she made. "I envy you," Ellynne said the next afternoon as they walked home from school. "You always seem so sure of yourself."

"I am sure of myself," Willie affirmed. "Best thing to be is sure of yourself — especially if you're black. That way, nobody else can tell you who you are or who you should be."

"Maybe so," Ellynne said. "But you're still lucky. Half the time, I'm not sure *what* I want."

"Oh, you're shy. That's part of your special aura. But you definitely know who Ellynne Aleese is and exactly what she wants."

Ellynne thought of Kip Russell and blushed. Could Willie tell how much she wanted to get to know Kip better? She was trying not to talk about him, and yet she couldn't resist asking questions.

"You and I are very different in some ways," Willie went on. As she talked, she waved her hands and thin gold bracelets rolled up and down her slim arms. "But we're more alike than different, I'm sure of that."

Ellynne looked at Willie speculatively. If only that were true. Ellynne would settle for one third of the poise and assurance that Willie Evans had. Ellynne smiled. "My mother always tells me to expect the best from life and I try. You're the first teenager I've ever met who really does seem to expect the best all the time."

Willie nodded emphatically. "Might as well aim high. Take men for instance. Time came for me to get a boyfriend and I looked around until I found the best. Come on in and I'll show you his picture."

Ellynne followed Willie into her home,

walked through the brilliantly colored living room with modern furniture and into Willie's bedroom. It was the second time she'd visited the Evans house, so she wasn't as startled by their splashy use of reds, oranges, and yellows. At first sight she'd been too shocked to decide, but now she looked around Willie's brilliant orange and yellow bedroom with the zebra-striped rug and black and white checked bedspread and decided she liked it.

She also liked the picture of the young man Willie held out for her to see. "He's a freshman at Stanford and you'll meet him Thanksgiving weekend. His name is Carl Robbins and one of these days, I'm going to be with him full-time."

Willie sounded so sure about her future that Ellynne didn't doubt it would come true. She said, "He must be a very special person."

"Yes." Willie nodded her head emphatically and sat down on her zebra-striped rug, crossing her legs in a half-lotus position.

They talked about men, love, careers, and books for the next two hours. Ellynne left Willie's house full of enthusiasm about her new friend and full of gratitude that they had so much in common. *It's going to be a wonderful year*, Ellynne promised herself, *a truly wonderful year*.

As she worked on her homework that evening, she found her thoughts straying back to Willie Evans and something that Willie had said. In a way, Willie's advice was a bit like her mother's, "Expect the best," only Willie seemed to attack the world more actively. "You've got to be absolutely clear about what you want," Willie had said. "Then you've got to go out and get it. Never let anything get in your way. Never give up. Never admit defeat. Make them drag you off the playing field, bloody, beaten, but unbowed."

Ellynne had laughed at Willie's exaggeration, but she suspected that behind Willie Evans' calm assurance lay a strength as tough as that of any football player's.

At the thought of football, Ellynne began to dream again of the day when Kip Russell would finally notice her. She saw him around school often, but so far he didn't seem to know that she was alive. He obviously didn't remember her because when she passed him in the halls, he never spoke. A couple of times she'd managed a smile but he'd looked straight through her.

It was all very well to expect the best as her mother advised, or even to go after him directly as she knew Willie would advise, but how was she to manage that until she registered with him? And how could she make him realize that she was there? As she made plans and spun dreams, they all seemed impractical. She couldn't just walk up to him and say, "Hi, I'm Ellynne . . ." No. That wouldn't work. She was too shy for that.

Science saved her from spending all evening worrying about Kip Russell. It was only the second week of school and the science teacher had loaded them with homework. After the bad beginning she'd had in that class, she wanted to do well. Ellynne turned her attention away from Kip Russell's slow smile, broad shoulders, and easy manner, to Mr. Morales' essay question about the future of scientific research in ordinary lives.

At eight-thirty the telephone rang and it was Merri. Ellynne was startled to hear from her even though Merri had been friendly in a distant way ever since the first day. Merri said, "Hi. Do you want to go to a party at my house after the game Friday night?"

"I'd like to," Ellynne began.

Before she could finish, Merri went on, "Good. You can ride to the game with me. It will give us a chance to get better acquainted. Have you done your essay yet?"

"I'm working on it."

"Well, for Pete's sake, tell me what you wrote. Would you read it to me? I can't think of anything at all."

Reluctantly, Ellynne read her essay to Merri. As she finished, she cautioned, "Don't write the same thing, Merri. Mr. Morales will check them carefully."

"I know that," Merri said disdainfully. "Thanks for the tips. I'll pick you up at six, Friday."

"That will be fine," Ellynne answered. "I'll check with my mother and let you know for sure tomorrow in science."

"Your mother! Do you have to check with her?"

Ellynne felt uncomfortable as she answered stiffly. "My mother and I always check out our plans with each other."

"Your mother must think that six and sixteen are the same," Merri said.

Ellynne couldn't think of a reply so she said, "Good luck on the essay," and hung up. Funny how Merri could manage to make her feel so young and silly so quickly. She was glad that Merri didn't know that she wasn't two weeks from fifteen. She had skipped a grade in elementary school and she'd always been younger than other kids. Before tonight, she'd never thought about it much, but her conversation with Merri made her feel that fifteen and five were the same.

Ellynne's mother was delighted that she was invited to a party and thought it was very nice of Merri to offer to drive her to the game. Judith Aleese looked at her daughter proudly and said, "I told you that you were the sort of person who would make friends quickly."

When Ellynne told Merri during science she'd be able to go with her and Merri nodded her head briefly, Ellynne wondered if Merri was sorry she'd asked her. Later, Ellynne asked Willie, "How will you get to Merri's party?" Willie would be riding to the game with the team because she was a cheerleader.

Willie said calmly, "I won't be going to Merri's party."

For one minute, Ellynne had a sickening thought. She asked, "You *were* invited?"

Willie grinned, "Oh yes, I was invited. Merri made a special point of it this time. I just don't want to go."

"Then I won't go," Ellynne said loyally.

Willie laughed at her. "Ellynne, don't imagine that anyone snubs me at the Merriweather house. They're always *extra* nice." Willie made a face and continued, "I suppose I'm supersensitive, but Mrs. Merriweather always makes such a point of telling me how *happy* she is that I could come and how *wonderful* she thinks it is that Merri and I are friends." Willie shrugged her shoulders and ended lamely, "The lady doth protest too much, methinks." Then she grinned and poked Ellynne in the ribs, "*Hamlet*, Act III, Scene 2."

"Yeah, you're smart, but the point is, I don't think I'm all that crazy about Merri either."

Willie raised her eyebrows. "But Merri's got something you want. Go get it, Kiddo."

Ellynne blushed as she tried to look as though she didn't know what Willie was talking about. She said, "It's true that I want to

48

meet lots of people and Merri's is the first party . . ."

"Can't kid me, Ellynne. Kip Russell will be at that party and you're a dummy if you aren't there too. You don't cut off your nose to spite my face, you know. Besides, I would rather sit home and write Carl a letter. That's my choice and I don't need any loyal supporters." As an afterthought, she added, "But thanks, anyway."

Ellynne said nothing more but she still felt funny about accepting the invitation from Merri. That night, she couldn't decide what to do and she sought advice from her friend, Lizzie.

Lizzie sounded surprised when she heard Ellynne's voice on the other end of the phone. She said, "Hang up. I'll call right back." It was a lot cheaper for Lizzie to call from Ohio because it was after eleven there and rates were lower then.

Lizzie listened carefully to Ellynne's dilemma, and when she finished telling her she responded, "So you don't know whether to stay home or go?"

"I'd like to go," Ellynne admitted. "Somehow, I have a feeling it's wrong, if the Merriweathers don't like blacks and Willie is my best friend."

"Sounds like Willie can take care of herself," Lizzie said. "It isn't as if Mrs. Merriweather has ever been rude or they didn't invite Willie."

Ellynne was somewhat relieved by Lizzie's advice but she still decided to check it out with her mother. Judith Aleese listened attentively and responded almost the same way Lizzie did. "Willie made a decision based on a feeling, and she's ready to accept that responsibility. She hasn't asked you to stay home and I think Willie knows she can take care of herself."

Ellynne kissed her mother on the forehead and said, "Thanks. Now that that's settled, I guess I can stick to the important decisions like what do I wear?"

Judith Aleese laughed and hugged her daughter tightly. "I only wish I believed you were kidding. It seems to me that you worry an awful lot about how you look these days."

Ellynne reminded her, "You were the one who pushed me to go on the diet."

"Yes. And I'm proud of the results. You did it just right — losing slowly and eating carefully. You look healthier, happier, and prettier. All that's wonderful, Ellie, just don't turn into one of those people who never think of anything but what shade of nail polish to wear."

Ellynne looked at her mother and noted that Judith Aleese was wearing the same navy blazer and blue checked slacks that she'd had on yesterday. She hadn't put on any lipstick since she started out at ten in the morning. Her mother was so interested in her studies that she seldom bothered with how she looked anymore. Privately, Ellynne thought that her mother was carrying things a bit too far.

She said, "I'll promise you, Mother. I won't turn into an empty-headed person, but don't expect me to look like a weirdo either."

Judith Aleese ran a hand over her straight hair that was pulled into a bun and asked mildly, "Is that how I look to you? Like a weirdo?"

"I wasn't talking about you," Ellynne said quickly. "I just mean I think it's normal for a girl my age to care about her appearance. And I'm normal."

Her mother smiled brightly and said, "Indeed you are, and I'm grateful for that."

Ellynne was relieved by her mother's comment, for a small voice inside her head was asking if she *was* becoming too looks-conscious.

Six

Ellynne was disappointed that she was the only passenger in Merri's car on the way to the football game. During the hour-long ride, Merri quizzed her about her old school, her old friends, and her family. When she heard that Ellynne's father was dead, she asked, "Is your mother looking for a new husband?"

Ellynne answered briefly, "My mother is in law school."

"How weird!" Merri exclaimed.

Ignoring the comment, Ellynne went on. "That's why we moved here. Mom wanted to practice in California and she needed a law school in the same state. Eventually, she hopes to move to Redlands and join my uncle's law firm."

Merri shook her head and said, "I know it's the thing for women to have careers, but *I* want to be a housewife. A couple of cute kids, a swimming pool, some nice friends, and a husband who takes care of me." She smiled slyly and said, "A doctor would be nice."

Ellynne felt her heart jump and her stomach lurch as she realized that Merri was probably including Kip Russell in her long-term plans, Kip, the brilliant science student who spent a lot of his spare time in Mr. Morales' laboratory. Ellynne supposed that he planned to become a doctor.

Ellynne tried to change the subject. "Those are great-looking pants you're wearing," she said.

Merri looked down at the white flannel pants and said, "They're O.K."

Ellynne wondered how anyone could be so nonchalant about such expensive and elegant pants. They probably cost more than everything Ellynne was wearing all tossed together. Merri made her feel awkward and plain as she sat beside her, and Ellynne wished again that someone else had been riding with them.

Merri asked, "You and Willie are really good friends?"

"Yes."

"Funny how she took to you so quickly. Willie's not like that. She's sort of stuck-up."

When Ellynne said nothing, Merri corrected herself. "Not exactly stuck-up, but distant. I mean, I try to be friendly but she won't even come to my parties. Always makes some excuse."

Again, Ellynne could think of nothing to say. Her face flooded with color, and she wished that Merri would just drop the subject.

"What was the real reason she didn't come?" Merri asked.

"She had to watch her cousins," Ellynne answered.

"Come off it," Merri said as she swung into the driveway leading onto the parking lot next to the football field. "The Evans family has enough money to buy thirty babysitters if Willie wanted to come."

Ellynne changed the subject again, "Oh, look, there are the cheerleaders."

Merri nodded brightly. "That's what I'll be next year," she said. Then she laid her hand on Ellynne's arm. "We should be friends, Ellynne. We could help each other. . . ."

It was then that Ellynne understood why she'd been invited to come to the party at Merri's house and why she'd been invited to ride in the car all alone with her. Merri wanted her to influence Willie to work for her to be a cheerleader. Willie had already explained to Ellynne that cheerleaders were chosen by a committee of teachers and businesswomen, but that the kids thought the old cheerleaders influenced the vote.

"I appreciate the fact that you invited me to your party," Ellynne said. "But I don't think I could say anything to Willie about you being a cheerleader next year. Besides, Willie says the old cheerleaders really don't have any pull."

Merri drew back quickly and laughed. "Don't know what you think I meant, Ellynne. I just meant I wanted to be friendly."

They dropped the subject and walked silently through the parking lot and into the football stadium. As they crossed beneath the scoreboard, Merri said, "Anyway, I don't really need Willie Evans' help. I'm good."

Ellynne looked down at the pert little girl beside her and said, "I'm sure you are." She wondered how Merri could seem so sweet and bubbly and say such cutting things.

Merri called out to a group of kids sitting about a third of the way up in the bleachers. Ellynne asked, "Shall we sit there?"

She laughed at Ellynne and said, "Of course not. We'll sit in the senior section."

"But we're not seniors," Ellynne protested.

"Doesn't matter," Merri answered. "Everyone knows about Kip and me and they won't say anything."

She led Ellynne down to the other section, carefully spreading her blanket on the bleacher so that her white flannel pants wouldn't get dirty. Ellynne felt uncomfortable about being in the section that was reserved for seniors, but she didn't dare protest to Merri. Merri had already let her know that she thought a lot of her ideas were peculiar.

No telling what she would say if she tried to persuade the girl to change to a less conspicuous seat.

Ellynne felt a bit better as the bleachers filled up and no one objected to Merri and her sitting there. People said hello and seemed friendly. One senior said, "Oh, you're the new girl that I've heard about."

Ellynne could tell by the way she said it that the things she'd heard were favorable. She was also pleased when Bruce Davidson came over and talked to her before the game began. As he left, Merri said, "Bruce is nice but kind of out of it. Did you want me to invite him to my party?"

Shaking her head, Ellynne pointed to the football field. "Here they come."

Both girls directed all their attention to the cheerleaders bouncing out onto the field. For the first time, Ellynne was glad they were sitting in the senior section. She was able to see everything.

Willie was the tallest cheerleader and she was usually in the center position. Even with a sprained ankle, she looked graceful and smooth as she jumped and stretched. As Ellynne watched, she tried to imagine what it would be like to be able to jump that high. She was thrilled when the crowd roared their approval of a new cheer that Willie had worked out last week.

Someday, I'd like to try, Ellynne thought,

but the thought faded out as the football team ran onto the field. The crowd jumped up, and as they sat down, Merri said, "I can do those cheers as well as any of those three."

Ellynne wondered if that was true. She sneaked a look at Merri who was leaning forward, watching the game with the intensity of a mad scientist plotting to overthrow the world.

After Ellynne located Kip Russell in the green jersey with the number 74 on the back, she watched him as closely as a second mad scientist.

The game went poorly, but Kip's playing seemed spectacular to Ellynne. He scored a 50-yard touchdown in the last minutes of the third quarter, but the score was still Long Beach 18–Redondo Beach 7.

At the third quarter, Merri asked Ellynne to go get some Cokes and she rose to get them even though she knew she'd miss part of the game. She wanted to see every move that Kip made just in case she got a chance to talk to him at the party. But Merri had said, "You get the Cokes. Kip would never forgive me if I missed this last quarter."

Ellynne bought two Cokes and carried them back to the bleachers where Merri was sitting. As she edged her way past the people in the row, Long Beach scored another touchdown and the people in the stands jumped to their feet, moaning and roaring with disap-

pointment. Someone knocked into her and Ellynne stumbled, spilling Coke all over Merri's
white flannel pants.

"You stupid thing!" Merri screamed.

"I'm sorry," Ellynne replied as the blood
drained out of her face and she watched the
sticky brown liquid roll down the front of
Merri's pants.

"You've ruined them," Merri screamed and
ran out of the bleachers toward the women's
restroom.

Ellynne followed along behind, repeating
over and over, "I'm sorry, I'm sorry."

Merri wouldn't speak to her or let her help
as she attempted to wash the sweet, sticky
Coke from her pants. When the worst of it
was gone, she looked down bitterly at the
soggy mess and said, "We'd better get home
so I can change for the party."

The girls walked to the car in a silence that
was broken only when Merri handed the keys
to Ellynne and said, "You'd better drive. My
pants will wrinkle even more if I try it."

"I can't," Ellynne admitted.

"Can't drive?" Merri asked incredulously.
"Why can't you drive?"

"I'm too young," Ellynne admitted. "I don't
have a license."

Merri looked at her as though she'd
crawled out from under a rock, but she said
nothing more, only climbed behind the wheel
of the car and started the engine.

An hour later, Merri was greeting guests, laughing merrily and pretending that the whole incident was funny. She would point to her blue velvet skirt and say, "It's just as well I changed into something more comfortable, don't you think?" Then she would tell the story of Ellynne's clumsiness one more time as Ellynne retreated farther and farther into the dark corners of the party.

Perhaps it was his own need for dark corners that made Kip Russell stumble into her and say, "I'm sorry."

By this time, Ellynne was so despondent that she couldn't manage more than a quiet, "It's all right, really."

"You're new, aren't you?" Kip said. "I'm Kip Russell."

"I know. I saw you play tonight."

Kip smiled and said, "Gruesome, wasn't it?"

"You were good." Ellynne's heart beat loudly as she looked up into Kip's eyes. This was the moment she'd dreamed of. If only he would ask her to dance, then every humiliating second of the evening would be worth it.

But Kip didn't ask her to dance. Instead, Merri called to him in a loud voice, "Come over here, Kip. We need you. And leave Ellynne alone. She's too young for you." Merri's voice tinkled out over the shadowed night. "In fact," she said cheerfully, "she's too young for words."

Kip grinned at her and turned to join Merri. Ellynne decided she couldn't bear another minute of this party. She went directly into the kitchen and dialed her home. When Judith Aleese answered, Ellynne said, "Mother, will you come for me? I don't feel very well." It was all she could do to keep from crying before she got out of the Merriweather house.

Seven

Ellynne felt so awful about the Friday night disaster that she really didn't want to talk about it when Lizzie called on Saturday. She'd managed to put her mother off by saying she didn't feel well. She'd told just a bit of the story to Willie who'd nodded dryly and changed the subject when she saw Ellynne blush.

Lizzie wasn't easily put off though. "Tell me about it," she begged. "What was the game like? Is Willie really good as a cheerleader? What about that girl you went with — Merri. Is she pretty?"

"Yes. Merri's pretty. In fact, Merri is what you call darling," Ellynne answered bitterly. "Her hair curls just right, her nose tilts up just right, her eyes twinkle, and her voice sounds like a little bell."

"You didn't like her," Lizzie said. "Well, so what. Did you meet any interesting people? Did you dance with your hero?"

"No, but I talked to him. He thinks I'm twelve. Merri told him I was, 'Too young for words.'"

Lizzie's voice was flat with disappointment. "I guess the party was a bust, huh?"

"Uh huh. Let's talk about your new job."

They chatted for thirty minutes, and when Lizzie hung up, she promised to call in two weeks. Her last bit of advice was, "Don't let the party get you down. It's only one party. There will be others."

But even though she knew Lizzie was right, Ellynne dreaded the prospect of going back to school on Monday. She was afraid Merri would continue to tell the story of the spilled Coke until every student at Redondo High School knew it. She was also afraid that everyone would think of her as "too young for words" after Merri finished telling the story.

In fact, Ellynne was more frightened as she dressed for school than she had been the first day. She walked into school as though she was in a dream, waiting for the first person she knew to speak to her. The people who went by her, brushing against her, seemed to ignore her.

Bruce Davidson stopped by her locker long enough to say, "I guess you're disappointed our team wasn't better."

Ellynne looked at him in amazement and shook her head. "No. I hadn't thought of that." She turned her back and pulled out her science book. That was the class Merri was in, and she dreaded it.

Bruce looked as if he would say more but Ellynne didn't give him a chance. She slammed the locker door and said, "See you."

It didn't cheer her up that Bruce Davidson was still friendly. What was it that Merri had said about him? Nice but out of it. Well, what could she expect? Birds of a feather flock together.

In science, Merri smiled and asked, "When did you leave the party? I looked around and you were gone."

"I didn't feel well," Ellynne answered shortly.

Merri laughed. "Well, I'm glad you're all right. My mom was worried about you. She said I was rude. Was I rude?"

"No. I'm sorry about the Coke." Ellynne didn't really want to apologize again but she couldn't help it. She felt worse when Merri waved her hand magnanimously and said, "That's all right."

Ellynne found that the kids treated her about the same as before. If she noted a slight drawing away, a slightly less friendly attitude, she couldn't be sure. Willie counseled her not to worry about it.

It was Thursday before Ellynne broke down and told Willie the whole dreadful story of the spilled Coke and the way Merri made her the butt of the too-often repeated story at the party. Willie listened quietly and then said, "I guess you feel like Merri has spoiled your chances at social success?"

Ellynne plucked at the fuzzy zebra-striped bedspread. She was sitting on the bed and Willie was curled in a huge wicker chair in the corner.

"I'm shy," Ellynne admitted. "When someone like Merri makes fun of me, I crumple."

Willie shook her head and said, "Can't crumple, Kiddo. If you crumple, they'll keep right at you. You got to learn to be brazen . . . brazen . . . that's female for brave." Willie began beating her chest and making Tarzan sounds.

Ellynne laughed. She said, "That's fine for you, Willie. And I notice that no one picks on you. But I don't know if I can do it."

Willie shook her head again and beat on her chest. "Me show you. Me brave. Me brazen."

Again Ellynne laughed, and then she admitted, "I'm just not a fighter. I can't imagine myself doing anything brave, let alone brazen."

"You do brave things," Willie said. "You came to a new school. You made new friends. You're doing fine, Kiddo. But the thing is, you've got to decide exactly what you want and go get it."

"I know what I want," Ellynne said. "I want to be popular. I want to have friends. I want to be invited to parties. I want to be invited out on dates."

"And the only thing that's stopping you is that Merri told everyone you're 'too young for words.' Well, are you going to let a little thing like that stop you?"

"I'll only be fifteen in two weeks," Ellynne said bitterly. "What if she finds out I'm only fifteen? And why did I have to apologize again today?"

Willie shrugged. "I guess because you have good manners. There's nothing wrong with good manners except they don't always work on people like Merri Merriweather. Know what I'd do?"

"No. What?" Ellynne teased. She knew that when Willie started giving advice, she'd get so wound up that she'd keep on for an hour.

"I'd be brazen. Instead of skulking around hoping that no one finds out that you're only fifteen, I'd give a great big birthday party so everyone knows that you don't consider a year's difference in age a social handicap. Invite everyone you want to know better. Leave Merri home."

Ellynne stared at her. "You mean announce that I'm only fifteen?"

"Why not? You can't help being fifteen any more than I can help being tall or black. Can you imagine what Merri and people like her would do to me if I let them?"

"Invite people I don't know?"

Willie grinned and nodded her head. "The direct approach. Why not?"

Ellynne nodded her head and said, "It might work. I'll ask my mother. A party might be expensive.

"Doesn't have to be. You could have ice cream and cake and soft drinks — something simple like that."

"Ice cream and cake!" Ellynne said incredulously. "They really would think I'm a baby."

"Have the party before the first dance of the year. Invite people for your birthday party and then they can go to the dance. It would work, believe me."

"When is the dance?"

Willie hopped out of the orange wicker chair and pulled her calendar off the wall. "The dance is November second," she said.

"My birthday is November fourth," Ellynne said. "It would work."

"That's settled," Willie said. She got out a pencil and paper. "Now, let's make the guest list. How many people will your apartment hold?"

As she waited for Ellynne to answer, Willie wrote the name Merri Merriweather at the top of the guest list and then drew a heavy black line through it. She looked up at Ellynne and grinned, saying, "That's voodoo for Miss Merriweather. Now tell me all the cute boys you've always wanted to get to know."

Ellynne took a deep breath and blurted, "Kip Russell." She could think of no more.

Willie wrote Kip's name down and waited. After a long time, she said gently, "Well, think of boys who have been nice to you or who you think look like good dancers. You can't have a party and invite just Kip." Her eyes twinkled. "At least, I'd save that party till next year."

Ellynne's mother said she thought a before-dance party would be a lovely idea and even offered extra money for refreshments. "No, thanks." Ellynne answered. "Willie and I are going to bake cookies and brownies. It's all part of the master plan to get to know more people."

Judith Aleese smiled absent-mindedly and said, "One of these days you'll find what you want to do with your life and you'll apply some of that marvelous drive to something worthwhile. Then you'll be a real winner!"

Though Ellynne knew it was intended as a compliment, she was hurt by her mother's comment. Why couldn't her mother see that right now, being popular was important? In fact, being popular was the most important thing in the world.

Ellynne bent over to take a bowl off the bottom shelf to mix the salad and winced in pain. Her mother asked, "What's wrong with your back?"

"Willie showed me how to do some cheers this afternoon. I feel stiff all over."

Judith Aleese laughed, shaking her head. "You and Willie are such smart people. I just don't understand how you can waste your time on silly stuff like that."

Ellynne changed the subject quickly, knowing there was absolutely no sense in trying to explain to her mother how important cheerleading was to her. The practice session with Willie had convinced her that it was hard work too.

Willie had shown her some limbering-up exercises and started showing her the simple jumps. Even with Willie's encouragement, Ellynne knew she would have to work very hard to get anywhere. She'd never been a particularly athletic youngster, and though she was now very slim and healthy, being overweight in her early teens hadn't helped her acquire many skills.

"I'll never learn to jump like that," she'd gasped when Willie leaped and then arched her body into a semi-circular shape.

"That's the Side Banana," Willie said. "You stick with me and you'll be doing that plus the Herkie." Here, she paused to jump high in the air, swing both arms out, and bend one leg while she extended the other one straight out.

Ellynne clapped her hands in admiration as Willie demonstrated jumps called the squat and tuck, then did a split in mid-air. She was careful not to let Ellynne try the jumps though, insisting that she begin with exercises for limbering-up and balance. She showed Ellynne how to practice the splits by using two chairs as supports as she stretched the muscles of her legs. Willie thought Ellynne had a chance to be a cheerleader next year, if she worked hard. Privately, Ellynne doubted it, but she was determined to give it a try. Starting tonight, she would spend 30 minutes a night on warm-up exercises and the simple moves that Willie showed her.

But Ellynne's thoughts weren't on cheerleading that evening, they were on a more immediate and more terrifying prospect. Willie and she had decided that Ellynne should ask Kip to her party tomorrow. "What will I say?" Ellynne had asked. Later, she had begged Willie to do it. When Willie was adamant, Ellynne had suggested that the telephone would be easier.

Nothing worked. The plan was that Ellynne would just walk right up to Kip Russell and say, "You're invited to my party. . . ."

Some plan, Ellynne said to herself as she tore the lettuce and chopped the green peppers for the salad. Even thinking of it made her get cold and shivery all over. What if he couldn't remember her? What if he said "no" and walked away? What if . . . ?

Ellynne woke up with so many *what-ifs* in

the morning that she considered staying home from school. She honestly couldn't tell if she was sick or just scared. Knowing that Willie would never forgive her if she backed out now, Ellynne dressed carefully and went to school even though she felt she was turning as hot and cold as a chicken on a spit.

When she saw Kip Russell walking down the hall all alone, she felt the blood drain away from her head. For a brief moment, she had a vision of fainting like the heroines in romantic novels of the past. What would Kip do if she just passed out in front of him? Step over her and keep on walking? Ellynne shook her head grimly at such silly thoughts and took a deep breath as she walked toward him.

"Hi, Kip," she said rather loudly.

Kip nodded and said, "Hi." He was obviously going to keep on walking.

She asked in a loud but trembling voice, "Wait a minute. I want to ask you something."

Kip stopped immediately and looked down at Ellynne. He was smiling slightly and he looked friendly and interested. It gave Ellynne courage to go on. "You may not remember me . . ."

"You're new," Kip supplied helpfully. "I met you at Merri's party."

"Yes," Ellynne sighed gratefully. At least he *remembered* her. "I'm new and I'm having a party. It's a birthday party — no presents — before the school dance. I hope you'll come. Willie and I planned the list and most of your friends will be there." She felt she'd been properly brazen until that last sentence, which seemed to float off into a small apology.

"I think I can come," Kip said. "Let you know for sure tomorrow."

"Fine," Ellynne said. Her hopes sank as she realized that Kip had just set it up so he could think of a good excuse. She was sure he'd come back tomorrow and tell her some story about having to study or take care of his sick grandmother. In their plans, Willie and she had decided that she should look very businesslike and tick him off on her list, urging him for an immediate decision since her apartment would only hold twenty, but all she could do was stand in his way, hugging her books to her chest, and look hopefully at him.

He had the most beautiful eyes she'd ever seen, and his smile made her want to stretch and purr like a kitten in the sunshine. She loved the way his red-brown hair curled around his ears, and now that she was so close to him, she could see that he had a bridge of freckles across his nose. She'd never known before how wonderful freckles could look.

"I work as a part-time checker at the Safeway Supermarket," Kip explained. "Usually, I can switch with someone else, but Friday nights are tough. I'll check with Dolores when I get there tonight. She owes me a couple of favors."

Ellynne nodded happily and smiled. "I hope you can make it," she said. "I really hope you can make it." She tried to look alluring as she smiled up at him but she had the feeling she looked silly.

He asked gently, "How many years?"

It took all of Ellynne's will power not to turn and run from the question. She knew she was blushing but she held her ground. "I'll be fifteen. That's a year younger than most juniors, but I'm a fast worker." The prepared response fell flat.

Kip grinned wider and said, "I knew you were just a kid, but I guess you're a smart kid." Then he added, "I'll only be seventeen when I graduate. I'm young for my class too."

The bell rang to go to class. It was in homeroom that Ellynne remembered she hadn't given Kip her name or address. *Never mind*, she told herself, *you did the important thing. You invited him, and tomorrow you can give him the details. It will be an excuse to talk to him again.*

But the next day, she didn't get a chance to talk to Kip at all. Merri accepted the invitation for both of them during science class. Merri said, "I think it's just wonderful of you to plan a party before the dance and you're brave to ask people you practically don't even know."

Ellynne couldn't tell if there was an edge of sarcasm in Merri's voice or not. She really didn't care. She hadn't invited Merri, but she'd been prepared for the possibility that Kip would. The important thing was that Kip would be at her party.

At the very least, he'd have to ask her to dance at least once at the dance after the party. She'd get a chance to be close to Kip Russell, a chance to be held in his arms, if only for a moment. The party was a wonderful idea, Ellynne decided. She smiled brilliantly at Merri and said, "I'm glad you and Kip will be there." She meant every word of it.

Eight

The money for the haircut came from an early birthday gift from her grandmother. The girl in the shop didn't charge Ellynne for the lightening since the bleach was really left over from the next-chair customer.

Ellynne looked in the mirror as she waited for her mother and Willie to arrive at the apartment. They were bringing the brownies from Willie's house, while Ellynne was getting her hair cut.

Yes, the blonde streak was perfect. It matched the sophisticated blunt cut that Ellynne chose. She turned her head slightly, holding the hand mirror up to see the way her heavy, light-brown hair hung straight down to her shoulders. It seemed to glow and glisten with health, and Ellynne knew she owed at least part of her hair's health to the high-protein diet she'd been following these many months.

In front, her hair was pulled straight across and held in place with a slim tortoise barrette. The tips of her hair turned up slightly as they hugged the smooth hollows below her cheekbones. The rich, light brown of her own color melted slowly into the lighter, brighter shade the beauty shop girl had offered her free of charge. "It will add excitement to your life," the beautician had promised.

Ellynne smiled at the lovely young woman in the mirror. Would she ever get used to looking like this? No doubt about it, she appeared slim, sophisticated, and elegant tonight. Even Kip Russell would be impressed — at least she hoped so.

The doorbell rang and Ellynne opened the door, helping her mother and Willie as they staggered beneath the weight of the refreshments. Judith Aleese said, "You made enough stuff for an army. There's more in the car." She put the brownies on the kitchen sink and left the apartment.

Ellynne was slightly disappointed that her mother hadn't even noticed her new haircut and color. Maybe it wasn't noticeable at all?

Willie noticed though. She took one look at Ellynne and hugged her. "You look terrific! Just terrific!"

Judith Aleese put the last cake on the sink and smiled pleasantly, saying, "Let me see." She turned around and looked at Ellyne. The smile turned cold and left her face. Her eyes narrowed and she said quietly, "You've lightened your hair, Eleanor Louise."

"Mom, call me Ellynne," Ellynne begged.

Willie looked from Ellyne to Judith Aleese and apparently sensing trouble coming, picked up a brownie and said, "I'll walk home. The exercise will help me get rid of some of these calories I'm consuming. See you later." She slipped out the door.

Ellynne defended herself from the unspoken attack. "It was just a little bit of color, Mom. The woman at the beauty parlor said it would brighten up the plain cut."

Judith Aleese went to the telephone and dialed the beauty parlor. She said firmly into the telephone, "My daughter is a minor — only fourteen — and she did not have permission to lighten her hair. I want you to know that you've lost two customers over this. Neither my daughter nor I will be back."

She slammed down the receiver and said, "I can't insist that you dye it back because tampering more with your hair would only make it worse. I'm very disappointed in you, Eleanor Louise. I thought you had better sense."

"Mom!" Ellynne said, trying to raise her voice. "I haven't done anything bad. All I did was get a light streak in my hair. Half the kids at Redondo High color their hair."

Judith Aleese looked at her daughter coldly. "Since when do you use the excuse, 'Everyone else is doing it'? You know that I am not interested in everyone else. I'm interested in you."

"I like the hair cut and I like the color. It achieves the effect . . ."

"Eleanor Louise, I'm geting very tired of hearing prattle about *effects* and such from you. This preoccupation with your looks and your social life is getting ridiculous. You seem to spend most of your time on that kind of nonsense."

Her mother's tone was cold and icy. Ellynne knew her mother was really mad. She could think of nothing to say except to defend herself in the unacceptable way, even though her mother's words upset her. "Mom, all kids my age are interested in their looks and their social life. It's normal."

But Judith Aleese was having none of that argument. She replied carefully, "I understand that a certain amount of concern for such things is normal, but I want you to make something of your life. You don't want to grow into one of those empty people who have nothing to talk about but surface things? You're a bright person, Ellie, you have your whole life in front of you. Don't let it slip away from you."

Ellynne had the feeling that her mother was thinking of herself as she had been at Ellynne's age. She knew that Judith Aleese felt some bitterness toward the high school that forced her to switch from the debate team to home economics to satisfy a rule. She knew that her mother felt she was pushed into choosing early marriage instead of college.

Judith Aleese sighed and patted her hair back with one hand as she began putting the cupcakes on the long trays. "Girls your age have so many advantages. You have the whole world in front of you. You can be anything at all." She picked up a chocolate frosted cupcake and said, "The world is your oyster. Success is your cupcake. Want one?"

Ellynne shook her head. "Not me. Those are for the people who can afford the calories."

Judith shook her head mockingly. "Such discipline. Now if you'd only apply the same discipline to your studies."

Ellynne was hurt and she replied sharply, "You agreed to encourage me on the weight thing — not make it hard for me. And I might remind you that I made the honor roll in my freshman and sophomore years."

"Sorry about the cupcake," Judith Aleese said lightly. "It's hard to remember you ever had a weight problem. But about your grades — can't rest on past glory, you know — how's it going this year?"

Ellynne blushed. She wished her mother hadn't asked. She grinned and answered honestly, "Having a bit of trouble in science." She didn't add that she was sure Mr. Morales was prejudiced against girls and that he obviously had labeled her a lamebrain that first day of school. Nor did she add that having

Merri in the class kept her from exhibiting her full potential. Truly, Ellynne was worried about science and felt guilty about her lack of success. Right now she was between a B and C. If she made a C, she wouldn't make the honor roll.

Ellynne said, "I have to change clothes. They'll be here any minute."

She looked around the living room of the apartment. It would hold the twenty people she'd invited without too much trouble. Luckily, her mother favored Oriental rugs and she'd been happy to let Ellynne and Willie lift the big one off the floor. So there was a corner for dancing and there was the record player. At the other side of the room, there was a long table laden with brownies, cookies, cupcakes, and sodas.

Ellynne was pleased with the effect. Yes, it was a simple and nice party and going to the dance afterwards would make it easier in every way. The neighbors wouldn't be able to complain about a party that lasted from seven-thirty to nine-thirty, and Ellynne wouldn't have the pressure of trying to entertain people for too long. They would come in, eat a lot, and go. As Willie predicted, all they'd remember the next day was that it was a good party.

Ellynne was dressed in a few minutes and she still liked her hair, despite her mother's objections. The slightly lighter glints made her rosy skin seem softer and the blusher she put on her cheekbones heightened that effect. When she pulled the soft blue sweater she'd chosen as her birthday present over her head, and run the brush through her blunt haircut, she smiled in the mirror. It was almost impossible to believe that this was the same shy Ellie Aleese who this time last year was sitting in her room on Saturday nights, writing in her diary a list of wishes, while she ate homemade fudge and worried about her figure and complexion.

She felt just wonderful as she opened the door for the first guest. They came in bunches after that, and within twenty minutes the apartment was full of laughing teenagers who were ploughing through the refreshments and the stack of records beside the record player.

One boy said, "These are *great* albums, Ellynne. Where did you get them?"

"I borrowed some," Ellynne admitted. The truth was that she'd borrowed all but two albums from Willie. Her own records were hidden in the case behind her mother's classical music. She knew that no one there would be interested in her collection of old blues.

Willie called for silence and then made a speech, "Now, folks, it's time to show our appreciation to our charming hostess. We all know that Ellynne went to a lot of trouble to put this spread together and we all know that the little girl is finally growing up." Ellynne blushed as Willie mentioned her age but she knew that it was part of Willie's "brazen" style.

"So the time has come to . . ."

The doorbell rang and Ellynne answered it. Kip Russell and Merri Merriweather were there. "Come on in," Ellynne said. "Willie is making a speech."

They joined the party and Ellynne was glad she had had an excuse not to talk to Kip for more than a moment. Of course, she was disappointed he'd brought Merri but it was almost overpowering to think of him here at all.

Willie was going on and on. ". . . So we are here to honor that charming hostess, that mystery girl, Ellynne Aleese."

She reached in her pocket and tossed a tiny package to Ellynne. Ellynne caught it and looked at Willie with dismay. She said, "You promised . . ."

Willie grinned and said, "Open it."

Ellynne pulled the paper from the tiny box and inside she found two thumb tacks and a note. The note read, "Hang in there, Mr. Morales."

Someone else tossed her a present. It turned out to be a small bottle of rose-colored water and a note that said, "For when you're feeling blue."

There were a lot of presents and each contained the small note that reminded Ellynne of the message inside a fortune cookie. Ellynne was sure that Willie had prepared most of the messages.

Kip's message read, "For a real doll." He had found an old Barbie doll dress and wrapped it up for her.

Ellynne turned to him and said, "Thanks a lot, Kip. You remind me a bit of Ken." Then she smiled her biggest smile at him.

Merri laughed too loudly and walked over to the refreshment table. She looked at all the cakes and cookies and said in a loud voice, "Your mother sure can bake."

Willie answered her, leaving the field open for Ellynne to go over to Kip and ask him to dance. When the music began, they fell into step and said nothing until the dance was over. Kip was a good dancer as Ellynne had expected. The more she saw of Kip Russell, the better she liked him.

She said, "I'm glad you could come to my party, Kip. I'd like to get to know you better." She smiled up at him again and tried to look expectant as she waited for his reply.

He could have said, "That would be nice," very vaguely and walked away. He could have said, "We will get to know each other," and patted her on the shoulder as if she was a silly little girl. She supposed he could have said, "No chance!" But what he did say was exactly what she'd hoped for.

Kip looked slightly surprised for a moment, then asked, "Would you like to go to the movies Sunday?"

Ellynne took a deep breath and sighed. "I'd love to," she said as Merri walked back to them.

"Love what?" Merri asked a bit too brightly.

Ellynne didn't have to answer because the telephone rang and Judith Aleese called from the kitchen, "Ellynne, it's Lizzie."

Ellynne frowned slightly. Lizzie would be calling to wish her a happy birthday. She hated to leave Kip so quickly but he couldn't go back on his invitation, no matter what. She went to the telephone and said, "Hi, Lizzie. Yes, the party's fine."

They chatted for just a few minutes, then Willie came over to the telephone and took it from Ellynne. She said, "Hi, Lizzie. I'm Willie, glad to meet you."

Behind Willie, a group of kids waited for their turn to say hello to Lizzie. By the time Ellynne got the telephone back, Lizzie had spoken to at least twelve people. Nervously, Ellynne wondered what she'd said. It would be just like Lizzie to make jokes about how much weight Ellynne had lost or how unpopular she'd been last year.

Lizzie may have sensed her fear or it may have been Lizzie's own shyness that made her say, "I'll hang up. You're in the middle of your party. We'll talk next week."

"No, no. Tell me what's happening in your

life," Ellynne said guiltily. As she talked to Lizzie, some of the kids began to leave for the dance. Ellynne waved good-bye to them. She would see them in a few minutes. It wasn't a big deal. Surely she could give Lizzie a few more minutes of her time. After all, she and Lizzie had been friends for a long, long time.

Merri and Kip came into the kitchen to say good-bye. Ellynne couldn't bear it. She interrupted Lizzie's tale about her hopes of working after school as well as Saturdays at the library. "I've got to go," she said. "Some of my guests are leaving."

Lizzie hung up quickly, after apologizing for talking so long. Ellynne felt awful about the loneliness in Lizzie's voice as she said, "I miss you, Ellie. I really miss you."

How much do I miss Lizzie? she wondered. Not very much, she had to admit. She was too busy thinking about her new friends and future to worry very much about the past.

"Who was that?" Merri asked.

"It was my best friend in Ohio, Lizzie Lawrence."

Merri made a face. "Weird name. Did she ever hear of Lizzie Borden?"

Kip said, "It must be hard to change to a new school in the middle of high school."

Merri laughed at the idea. "It's not hard for Ellynne. She's doing fine."

Ellynne ignored Merri and said to Kip, "It's hard sometimes, but people have been nice to me."

"What's Lizzie like?" Merri asked suddenly. "Is she cute?"

Ellynne thought about Lizzie's looks. Would Merri think she was cute? No. No way that Lizzie Lawrence would compare in looks to a girl like Merri Merriweather. Ellynne said softly, "Lizzie's got a good personality. She's nice-looking and a good friend."

"Let's see her picture," Merri demanded.

Ellynne couldn't understand why Merri was pushing the idea of Lizzie so hard. Was it just to distract Kip or was it because she sensed something uneasy in Ellynne when she spoke of Lizzie Lawrence? Ellynne didn't know and she recognized the possibility that it could be no more than that Merri was curious about Lizzie. Whatever it was, Ellynne had no intention of showing anyone Lizzie's photo.

"Come on," Merri urged. "Get out the photo album and show us your old school pictures. Were you in a lot of clubs last year?"

That's when Ellynne became sure that Merri was doing this to make her uncomfortable. She said only, "It's time to go to the dance. It will be over at twelve."

Merri sniffed. "Who cares? All the really important kids are right here." She looked around the room and asked shrewdly, "Willie help you make out the guest list?"

Kip laughed and took Merri's arm. "You make Ellynne sound like a social climber or something. Come on, Merri. It's time to go."

Ellynne looked at Kip gratefully. He had good manners and he was a sensitive person as well as being handsome, talented, smart, and a good athlete. In fact, the infatuation she'd felt for Kip Russell the first night was definitely confirmed after having a chance to spend some time with him.

She was very glad she'd given this party. She was also very glad that Kip had asked her to the movies on Sunday evening. So far, everything was working wonderfully well.

As Kip and Merri turned to leave, Willie called from the living room, "Ellynne, come on in."

Ellynne followed Kip and Merri to the door, then turned back to the crowd in the living room. Willie was laughing and pointing to the three girls who were lined up with their arms around each other, kicking high in the air, like Radio City Music Hall Rockettes. Willie said, "Get in the contest, Ellynne. I'm the judge."

"What kind of a contest?" Ellynne asked.

"Cheerleader," people cried simultaneously.

The music from the record player was almost full volume. Ellynne fell into step with the other three girls. They twisted their bodies to the right, kicking high, and then to the left. As they twisted, they chanted,

> Good, better, best,
> We'll put them to the test.
> 'Cause good we are
> And better we'll be,
> We're the best!
> Yes sir-ree!

As the cheer ended, Ellynne jumped high into the air, leaving the other three girls behind. One accused, "You've been practicing." Ellynne nodded and blushed.

Willie pointed her slim brown finger at Ellynne and said, "The Winner and Next Cheerleader of the World, Ms. Ellynne Aleese."

Some of the kids clapped and Ellynne smiled. She hadn't been sure she wanted all that attention, but now she knew she did. It felt great to have people clapping for her. *Wouldn't it be wonderful*, she thought. Right then and there, she made up her mind to work harder than anyone. If determination could do the job, she would be a cheerleader next year. She was sure of that.

Ellynne knew her face was flushed from the exercise and pride. She felt very happy. If only what Willie predicted would come true! But why not? Other dreams had come true this evening. She actually had a date with Kip Russell for Sunday night.

The other girls didn't like Willie's decision even though the contest had been a joke. As they left, Helen Harvey said loud enough for Ellynne to hear, "Merri's right. She is pushy."

Ellynne tried not to let the remark hurt her. She supposed that success always engendered a certain amount of envy and she knew that Helen was envious of her success this night. Still, she would have to be careful in the future not to be too obvious. If she'd made some friends tonight, she'd made a couple of enemies also.

As she pulled on her coat to go to the dance, she thought that it was too bad life was so complicated. "Expect the best!" her mother said. "Brazen is the best!" Willie said. Yet, she had made Merri and Helen angry and she had a small suspicion that her date with Kip was a result of his feeling sorry for her. It was hard to know exactly what was the right thing to do. Ellynne sighed to herself as she closed the door and walked out into the cold November evening.

Nine

Kip was thirty-seven minutes late for their date, and by the time he got there, Ellynne was tied up as tight as a pretzel. *Act nonchalant*, she told herself as he explained that he'd misjudged the time it would take to get back from a science exhibit at the museum in Los Angeles.

"I would have been all right," Kip finished apologetically, "if someone hadn't called for help in science as I was walking out the door. This person is close to failing the course so I couldn't say no."

"Of course not," Ellynne said in a voice that sounded much brighter than she felt. She was sure the person who'd called was Merri and that didn't make her feel a bit better about the fact that they were going to miss the first fifteen minutes of the movie.

All the way to the theater, Ellynne chattered about school, about movies, and about football. Kip seemed only to be half-listening. The less interested he seemed, the more Ellynne talked. By the time they got to the theater, Ellynne felt just like one of those wind-up dolls with the "too-fast" voices. Even though she knew she was turning him off with the nervous, tense prattle, she was powerless to stop.

Kip watched the movie and said nothing to her except at intermission when he asked, "Do you want popcorn?"

"No, but I'll go with you," Ellynne said brightly.

He shook his head. "I'll be right back. I have to make a phone call. You save our seats."

Crushed by his rejection, Ellynne felt the blood drain from her face as she leaned back in the seat. She felt like a fool as she realized that Kip wasn't really interested in her at all. *He's going to call Merri*, she thought, and the idea gave her such sharp pain that she actually gasped.

There were tears in her eyes as she told herself she'd been a fool to think that anyone like Kip Russell would be seriously interested in her. She wanted to get up and run out of the theater right then, but, of course, she couldn't.

On the way home from the movies, she didn't chatter. In fact, she didn't say anything at all. When Kip asked her how she liked the second film, she said, "Fine," and that was the end of the conversation.

This time, the air was silent and heavy as Ellynne watched the street lights speed by her. *He's taking me straight home*, Ellynne thought. *This is the first and last date with Kip Russell.* One part of her screamed at herself, *Do something!* But there was nothing to do. She felt paralyzed with fear and depression. She could think of nothing at all. If she began talking again, she knew she would only make things worse.

At the door, she asked, "Would you like to come in for leftover brownies and a Coke?" That was part of her plan B that she'd worked out back earlier today when she'd held out hope for this date.

Surprising her, Kip said, "Sure."

Ellynne felt like such a deadweight dunce that she was almost sorry Kip had accepted her proposal. She unlocked the door, switched on the light, and said, "My mom will be in soon. She went to a dinner party at one of her professor's houses."

"Your mother must be an interesting woman."

Ellynne nodded, grateful for a safe subject. "She is, I guess. After I went to kindergarten, she started taking courses at the community college. By the time I was ten, she had her degree, and when Dad died, she decided to go to law school."

She took a Coke from the refrigerator for him. For herself, she took a low-calorie soda.

No matter what Kip thought of her, she wasn't going to slip into drinking things that would make her fat. Nothing was worth putting on the old weight.

If Kip noticed that her drink was different, he said nothing. He walked into the living room and began looking through the records stacked beside the record player.

Ellynne felt a sinking feeling. Now Kip would realize that none of the popular music she'd played at the party was really hers. This stack was a mixture of her mother's classical and her own blues collection. It was just one more way that would prove how unacceptable, how different she was.

Kip looked up and her and asked, "Are these John Lee Hooker records your mother's?"

"No," Ellynne answered. "They're mine. I collect blues."

For the first time all evening, Kip's face looked genuinely interested. His blue eyes were almost excited as he asked, "Do you have any Bessie Smith?"

She nodded. "I even have a couple of originals."

"You're kidding?" It was as if she had announced she had a million dollars stacked in the coat closet.

"You're interested in blues?" she asked. She could barely dare to hope that such a thing could be true.

Kip nodded. He said, "Mostly I collect jazz from the thirties and forties. I've got big band stuff. Glenn Miller, Bob Crosby, Count Basie. I guess your stuff is older," he added shyly.

"My stuff is sadder," she teased. "Want to hear the Bessie Smith?"

Kip bit into the brownie he was holding, sat down on the couch, and settled back to spend some time. Ellynne didn't remind him of the test he had been so worried about. She just pulled out record after record that he might enjoy.

Between discs, he asked her about her father, her old school, and how she liked Redondo High.

Ellynne answered simply, telling the truth, but skipping over the parts that she wasn't comfortable telling. She didn't tell him that her interest in blues developed as a substitute for feeling part of the popular crowd. She didn't tell him how often she'd sat in her apartment alone on Saturday nights and listened to Billie Holiday or Ida Mae Cox sing the blues while she ate junk foods and worried about not being popular.

The story Ellynne painted was a prettier picture than that. She told of her sense of loss when her father died and how she'd picked up his interest in blues to help her feel close to his memory. She told of her affection for the women singers who seemed so close to her feelings when her father was ill.

When Kip asked if she missed her old school much, Ellynne answered truthfully. "I miss my friend Lizzie some, and, of course, I miss the seasons. It would be snowing now," Ellynne continued softly. "I'd be getting my skis ready for the Thanksgiving vacation just in case there would be enough snow. . . ."

"I guess you miss it," Kip said.

She shook her head. "Not as much as you might think. I love the beach, the sunshine. I love Redondo High. The kids are friendly and fun."

"Maybe you'll get a chance to go skiing," Kip said. "It's only a couple of hours to Mt. Baldy. You can rent equipment here in town."

"I'd like that," Ellynne said. She hoped it was a promise that included him.

As though he understood her unspoken question, Kip explained, "I have football and work besides school. That keeps me busy most of the time. I need the job to get to college." He made a face. "With a football team like ours, there's not much chance of an athletic scholarship."

"But you're good," Ellynne said loyally. It was true. Kip was good but the team had yet to win a game.

Kip shrugged. "I'm not great, just competent. Too bad the team's not better. But so what? I'll get to a good college.

"Of course you will," Ellynne said. She was listening to the mellow voice of Dinah

Washington sing, "Be good to him, he's your man," and she was feeling good. Her date with Kip hadn't been a total flop after all. He seemed happy enough sitting on her couch, drinking a soda, and talking with her. Funny how much easier when you had something in common with someone.

He was just leaving as Judith Aleese came in. He shook her hand and said, "I've been enjoying your record collection. Perhaps one of these days Ellynne can come to my house and hear my big band collection."

Judith was impressed by Kip's manners, and the minute he went out the door, she said so. "It's wonderful to meet a young man who has good manners."

Ellynne nodded her head dreamily. She hugged the Bessie Smith album close to her breast and said, "He said he might take me skiing. He said he'd invite me to hear his records."

Judith shook her head and teased, "You look moon-struck. Did you get your science homework done this weekend?"

"Of course," Ellynne answered haughtily. She hoped she never got as old as her mother, who didn't seem to have an ounce of romance left in her body. She was annoyed with her mother for breaking her mood with cold reality, and it didn't help to know she hadn't quite told her mother the truth. The science homework was only half-done and it was too late now. She'd try and finish it in homeroom tomorrow. If not, she could only hope that Mr. Morales would skim-read.

She certainly wasn't going to try to do it now. It was almost midnight and she wanted to look beautiful when she got to school tomorrow. No, now she would go to her room, brush her hair, put cream on her face, and get into bed.

Tonight, she would dream only the best of dreams. Tonight, she would dream that Kip Russell was holding her in his arms. She would dream that Kip was holding her very close and whispering in her ear that he loved her. She would dream that Kip was swearing his undying devotion. She would dream that she was looking up into his eyes and saying, "I love you too." And, of course, she would dream that he invited her to the Homecoming Dance, which was only ten days away.

Ten

But dreams are not daytime things, and Ellynne's dreams were shattered at lunch the next day. All morning she'd hugged the thought of Kip Russell close. When she sat down next to Willie at lunch, she'd been so happy.

"You had fun?" Willie asked.

Ellynne nodded dreamily and looked around the cafeteria for Kip Russell. He usually worked in the science lab, but sometimes he came down for sandwiches to take back. Sometimes he stopped and chatted for a second.

She found Kip easily. His lean good looks, his broad shoulders, and his wonderful laugh made him easy to spot in any crowd. At first when she saw him, she felt wonderful, but she soon realized that he wasn't alone. Merri Merriweather was walking beside him!

Ellynne's face went white, her heart sank, and she ducked her head, looking down at the food in front of her. Why had she been such a fool as to think that Kip was really interested in her? After all, he was Merri's boyfriend, wasn't he?

They came laughing through the crowd of kids. Merri was looking up at Kip, batting her blue eyes as though they were electronic devices. As they neared her, Ellynne heard Merri's tinkling little laugh and then she heard her say, "Oh, Kip, you are just the funniest guy."

Ellynne pushed the salad around in the plastic container and wished she could fly away from this table. At that moment, she would have given anything at all to be back in Ohio. Why did she *ever* think she could compete with Merri Merriweather? She felt awful.

Merri slid into the seat across from her. Ellynne lifted her head and said in a shattered voice, "Hi, Kip."

Kip nodded and smiled at her. Merri cut across and asked him, "Do you think I should wear my yellow dress or my white dress to the dance?"

Kip said lightly, "Either. You always look fine." Then he put his hand lightly on Ellynne's shoulder and smiled again. He asked, "How are you doing?"

Merri's face clouded for a second, then she opened her eyes wider, and asked in a sweet, cheerful voice, "But which dress do *you* like best, Kip? Mama won't let me have a new one and I want to look nice. I want to please *you*."

Kip smiled and said, "Wear the yellow one. I like that." He nodded to Willie and left the table before anyone could say anything else.

Ellynne's shoulder felt warm and almost burned where Kip had touched her. Why was it that the touch of a certain boy could turn you into Jello? Ellynne thought of the answer her mother would give her: *Chemistry*. Well, maybe it was just chemistry, but she knew she would never love anyone the way she loved Kip Russell.

Maybe Merri read her thoughts. The minute Kip was out of hearing range, Merri said to Ellynne, "You have a nice record collection, I hear." Her voice was amused and Ellynne felt hot and cold as Merri went on. "Kip told me he was taking you to the movies. He tells me *everything*. After all, Kip and I have been going together since eighth grade."

Ellynne could think of absolutely nothing to say.

Willie piped up. "You may be going together, but Kip obviously considers himself a free agent. Or did he ask your permission to date Ellynne?"

Merri's eyes narrowed and she said, "Kip took Ellynne out one time. But he's mine. He's been mine since eighth grade."

"You make Kip sound like a new bracelet

or a book you don't want to loan," Ellynne said. She was surprised and proud of herself for speaking up to Merri.

"Listen, Miss New-Girl, don't think you can come in here and take whatever you want. Besides, Kip thinks you're dull. He told me so. Dull as dishwater, that was his expression."

"I don't believe you," Ellynne said. But she *did* believe her. After all, she had been dull last night. The very fact that she was close to Kip had made her freeze. And Kip must like cheerful, cute girls because he liked Merri. When Kip was around, Merri was a darling person.

Ellynne looked across the table at Merri. Right this minute, she didn't look darling at all. Her face looked ugly. *I wish Kip could see her now*, Ellynne thought. Then she brushed the thought aside. It did no good to think of Kip as a bone to be fought over. *People are not property*, she reminded herself.

Lunch ended in silence. That evening, Ellynne wrote in her journal about the wonderful date she'd had with Kip Russell. She tried not to let the fact that he was taking Merri to the Homecoming Dance upset her. *It had been a wonderful evening*, she told herself.

At nine-thirty, Ellynne sighed and turned off the light. Thinking positively was hard work sometimes. She couldn't help comparing herself to Merri and she couldn't help wishing she were more effervescent. Merri was always so bright and bubbly around Kip — no wonder he dated her. Ellynne was really sorry she'd told Kip all that sad stuff about feeling so alone when her dad died. She made herself a promise to stay cheerful from now on, no matter what.

It was Thursday before she saw Kip again. He stopped her in the hallway and asked, "Want to come to my place Sunday night? We could have pizza and listen to records." He added, "My mother will be home."

Ellynne blushed at the thought he would have to tell her that. One of the things that had first attracted her to Kip was his kind, gentle manners. She really admired him for that. It wasn't easy for a football player who was as good-looking as Kip not to fall into the macho syndrome.

"I'd love it," Ellynne said.

The weekend wasn't so bad because she had Sunday evening to look forward to. It hurt a bit to imagine Kip and Merri out together on Saturday night, but she kept busy, reading a new novel and entertaining her mother's friends. Judith Aleese was developing a social life of her own in this new town. Ellynne noted with mild amusement that one of the professors of law who came to dinner seemed more than professionally interested in her mother.

On Sunday night, Kip picked her up at seven-thirty and brought her home at ten. It was a pleasant evening spent listening to records. About the only thing surprising was that Kip's mother served a plate of celery and carrot sticks to munch on. Ellynne was grateful until Kip said, "Merri said you were always on a diet, so I thought you might like these better than pie."

Ellynne was so tongue-tied that she just laughed and said, "Crazy about carrots." She would have gladly killed Merri if she could have gotten her hands on her.

Kip said, "I eat everything in sight. Get all that exercise, you know."

He turned the Blind Lemon Jefferson record and said, "Listen to his phrasing. Lou Rawls copied it forty years later."

Ellynne got so interested in the music she forgot to be mad at Merri, or self-conscious about not eating, or trying to make a good impression, or worrying about the fact that Kip was taking someone else to the dance.

When she left, she said, "I had a good time," and really meant it.

When she got home, she found a note from her mother that said, "Bruce Davidson called. He'll see you tomorrow in school."

Ellynne couldn't imagine what Bruce wanted. She barely knew him. All she knew for sure was that he was a friend of Willie's boyfriend and a basketball player. He was a nice fellow and she dared to hope that he wanted to ask her out. How would that be? Would it make Kip jealous?

Sure enough Bruce stopped her in the hall at school and asked her if she wanted to go to the Homecoming Dance. He said, "I know it's late notice but I wasn't sure I was going to be in town."

"That's funny, I'm not sure I'm going to be in town," she answered smoothly. "May I let you know tomorrow?" It was easy to be cool and unruffled as long as it wasn't Kip Russell she was talking with.

The truth was, she didn't know whether she wanted to go to the dance with Bruce Davidson or not. She couldn't decide if it would be better or worse for her image with Kip. She wanted to talk to Willie, to discuss strategy, but Willie really was out of town. She had flown with her family to a three-day psychiatric conference in Taos, New Mexico.

There really wasn't anyone else to ask but Lizzie. That evening, she dialed Ohio and told her old-time best friend her problem. Lizzie listened quietly and then she said, "You should go to the dance with Bruce. You've never been to a Homecoming Dance and you may never be invited again."

Lizzie sounded plaintive as she talked, and Ellynne realized that she had never been invited to *any* dance. Ellynne was torn between pity for her friend and irritation that she set her sights so low. She wanted to tell Lizzie how easy it was to aim for social success. But was it really easy? Ellynne knew she'd put a lot of work into planning how to act, how to appear, what to say, and what to wear. Somehow, she knew that Lizzie would never care enough about being popular to do all that.

"Thanks, Lizzie," she said and hung up the phone. She had wasted her money calling Ohio. Lizzie and she were in different worlds now, and Lizzie simply didn't understand.

When Judith Aleese walked in the door at ten, Ellynne made her cup of coffee and said, "A boy named Bruce Davidson asked me to the Homecoming Dance."

Judith kicked off her shoes and sipped the coffee gratefully. "That's nice," she said. "Wow, I'm tired. I struggled through those court decisions until my eyes wouldn't focus. Still haven't found exactly the right precedent."

"I don't know if I should accept," Ellynne said. "Kip is taking Merri and I don't know if it would look better to be at the dance with a boy I don't like or stay home."

Judith frowned and put the coffee cup down. "What did I do to have a daughter who thinks of nothing but boys, clothes, and dances? Don't you know that times are changing, child?"

Though her mother's voice was light and teasing, Ellynne knew she was serious. She searched for the right words to explain. "Mom, I know times are changing, but I have to be who I am. Someday, I'll be grown up and I want to look back on my high school days as happy ones. I want to be popular, Mom. Is there anything wrong with that?"

Her mother shook her head. "It's wrong when you place superficial values first, Ellie. I've been waiting for you to get over this silly phase and get back to being your own person. I'm getting tired of waiting."

"My grades are good."

"Your grades are good — not spectacular. You could be a spectacular student if you tried." Judith Aleese shook her head again and smiled a tired smile. "I see your opportunities and I know how rich they are. I see you brooding about unimportant things and I worry. Next thing I know, you'll want to be a cheerleader or something."

Ellynne's face flushed. How did her mother know? She had been practicing the jumps ever since Willie started to show her the routines. She did want to be a cheerleader, but it was such a wonderful dream she didn't dare say it aloud. Yet she wondered if she was just a superficial girl.

"Will you buy me a new dress for the dance?" Ellynne asked quietly, pushing the thought away. She saw no sense in pursuing this conversation with her mother. Her mother was tired and she would never understand.

"I'll pay half," Judith Aleese answered. "But you'll have to shop for it yourself. I'll be working every night this week."

Ellynne nodded. "Willie will help me on Thursday. The dance is Friday night so that doesn't leave me much time, but I'm sure I can find something."

Her mother obviously appreciated the fact that Ellynne backed off from the discussion. She stood up, kissed Ellynne on the forehead, and said, "It's wonderful that you're keeping your weight down. Last year this time, we wouldn't have been able to find a dress that you liked if you started shopping a month ahead of time."

Ellynne smiled and agreed. "Losing that weight changed my life."

A flicker of worry passed across her mother's face. "Yes, it did. I only hope it changed it for the better."

Eleven

Ellynne found a soft, moss green dress with simple lines and a full skirt that swirled around her legs as she walked. The dress was mid-calf length and she wore beige sandals that she borrowed from Willie.

She felt overdressed and stiff as she waited for her date. No matter how many times she looked at her reflection in the glass, she couldn't seem to accept that the slim, pretty girl who looked back at her was really Ellynne Aleese — former teenage nothing.

But no matter how impervious she was to the reflection in the glass, she had to acknowledge Bruce Davidson's enthusiastic compliments. He seemed very nervous as he handed her scarlet flowers, saying, "You look beautiful."

All the way to pick up Willie and her boyfriend, Bruce repeated the same thing: "You look beautiful."

By the time they got to the Evans house, Ellynne felt good about her appearance and mildly amused by Bruce's obvious crush on her. She practiced flirting with him, looking him directly in the eye, blinking her darkened lashes, and saying things like, "You must be so impatient to have football over and have the basketball season start. I just love basketball." Bruce was on the basketball team.

Bruce stumbled over his feet as he got out of the car to open the car door for her. Ellynne knew it was nervousness and she thoroughly enjoyed the knowledge. It felt good to have someone nervous about impressing *her* for a change. She flirted with him all the way to the dance. When he asked her for the first dance of the evening, she said in a soft, seductive voice, "I'd just love to."

Willie looked up sharply at the sound of her voice. When the dance was over, Bruce went for Cokes and Willie said, "You've got that guy falling all over himself. Are you interested in him?"

"Bruce? No. You know I'm interested in Kip Russell."

"Then lay off the poor guy, for Pete's sake. It's not nice for a beautiful woman to play with men as though they were toys. You want to grow up to be like one of those dippy dames in the movies? The old stars who brag about how many men have committed suicide over them?"

Ellynne laughed at the idea but she realized that Willie wasn't really kidding. *I'm beautiful enough to break hearts*, Ellynne thought. For the first time since she'd lost all that weight and changed her appearance, Ellynne understood how beautiful she really was. There was power attached to beauty.

When Bruce came back with the Cokes, she was the regular Ellynne again, saying simply, "Thanks, Bruce."

From that point on, she didn't flirt with Bruce. Nor did she flirt with any of the other young men who asked her to dance. Several of them told her she looked nice and to each she answered, "Thank you."

No more batting eyelashes or smiling slow, seductive smiles, but she had a good time anyway. As she danced and laughed, she almost forgot about Kip and Merri on the other side of the room. After all, she was fifteen years old and at her very first Homecoming Dance. It was a once-in-a-lifetime occasion and she didn't intend to spoil it wishing she were with another boy. She was almost cool when Kip walked across the room to ask her to dance. It was a slow dance and she melted into his arms as easily and gracefully as if they had been dancing together for years.

"You're a good dancer," he said. "Must come from listening to all those blues."

"I wonder what it was like — dancing to the big bands."

"Great, I guess. I wish that were Count Basie sitting up there," Kip answered as he twirled her around.

Ellynne felt very pretty and very happy as she turned to the music. She was dancing with the man of her dreams, wearing a beautiful dress, and having a wonderful time. She smiled a small smile at herself. She was the girl who had thought of staying home!

"Want to go to the movies next Saturday?" Kip asked.

Ellynne leaned her head against his shoulder as she murmured, "I'd love to." So she wasn't always going to be second-best girl. He'd invited her out on Saturday night. Would he take out Merri on Sunday? Maybe, maybe not. The important thing was that he was taking her out on Saturday.

As she leaned against his shoulder, she pretended to herself that Kip had taken her to the dance. Soon, he would be taking her home. They would stop for coffee and hamburgers somewhere and then he would lead her up the steps to her house. He would take her in his arms and crush her to him. He would kiss her madly, passionately, as he proclaimed his love. He would . . .

Her dream was shattered as he said, "I've been switched to Friday nights and all day Sunday at the supermarket. It means more work for me, but I'm glad to have the money."

"You don't think you can get a football scholarship?"

Kip laughed shortly. "No. I'm good — but not great, and we haven't won a game."

"I'm so sorry. It's a shame you couldn't have had a good team to play on."

"It will be fine," Kip said confidently. "I've got my part-time job. I can get a government loan, so I'll get along wherever I go."

The music stopped and Kip walked her across the dance floor. She hoped he would stay with her but she knew Kip well enough by now to know that was impossible. His manners were too good.

He said seriously, "I'm going to meet a lot of obstacles in my life, everyone does. This no-scholarship-to-college is just an obstacle. Know what I read once?"

"No. What?"

"I read that we are the result of the way we handle the obstacles we meet. In other words, what happens to us isn't as important as how we handle what happens to us. Get it?"

Ellynne thought about her own life. She could have stayed home and felt sorry for herself because Kip invited Merri to the dance. She'd handled that obstacle, and here she was, having a solid and serious conversation with Kip, a conversation she was sure he'd never have with Merri.

She said, "I think I understand that. My mom's gone a lot and I'm alone. If I stay home and feel sorry for myself, eating fudge and reading novels, I get fat. If I get out and do things, then I get happy."

Kip nodded and then laughed. "Not that you ever have to worry about getting fat. But that's the idea." He smiled down at her, his hand squeezing hers, and said, "Thanks for the dance, Ellynne. See you Saturday night."

As Ellynne turned back to her friends, she thought, *I'm so glad I came to the dance. I'm having a wonderful time.*

Twelve

They stopped for hamburgers and Cokes after the dance, so it was nearly two when Ellynne got home. She was amazed to find her mother sitting in a chair, sound asleep, with a high school album spread out on her lap.

Ellynne kissed her mother lightly on the forehead and said, "Mom, it's time to get up."

Judith Aleese woke suddenly, sat up in the chair, and stretched her arms out wide. She said, "I wanted to wait up for you and I wanted to sleep so I guess I compromised."

"What time do you have to go to the library tomorrow?" Ellynne asked in a chiding voice. Her mother was working too hard, she was sure of that. Little lines were beginning to appear around the corners of Judith Aleese's eyes and mouth.

"I wanted to show you this," Judith Aleese said. She opened the high school annual in front of her to a picture of some girls and boys standing in front of a sign that said "National Scholarship Society." "Can you find your mother?"

"That's easy," Ellynne said. She pointed to the slim blonde with the ponytail in the front row. Her mother hadn't really changed much in twenty-three years. The main difference was that the old clothes looked funny.

Judith Aleese smiled. "I was cleaning out a file cabinet so I'd have room for some new research data, and I found this album. That was 1960. I was sixteen years old," she said softly.

"You were pretty."

Her mother shook her head. "I didn't feel pretty. Funny how you push thoughts and feelings away when you get older. I've been criticizing you for worrying too much about your appearance, but it was really myself I was criticizing. I was in a constant stew about how I looked." Judith Aleese laughed and pointed to her shoes. "See those? I remember how much they cost, what shop I bought them in, and what popular girl bought them first."

She put her arm around Ellynne and hugged her. "Ellie, I owe you an apology. As long as your grades stay high enough to get you into a good college, I have no complaints. You're only young once, so dance, laugh, and have as much fun as you can."

"You weren't very happy when you were a kid, were you?" Ellynne asked.

Judith Aleese rubbed her eyes. "I was miserable all the time. I wanted to please my parents, my teachers, the kids in my class. I never thought about pleasing *me*."

"Why didn't you go to college? You were in the scholarship society, so your grades were good enough."

Judith Aleese shrugged. "My folks thought it was important for boys to go to school, but they weren't too concerned about their daughters. I went to a community college for a while and then my dad got sick. It seemed more important to help at home and work than go on with an education. I had no real plans."

Ellynne shook her head at the thought of her mother with "no real plans." Ever since she could remember, Judith Aleese had been taking night courses and working on projects that took real brains.

"I didn't stay up till two in the morning to talk about me," Judith Aleese said lightly. "I stayed up to talk about your dance. Tell me all about it."

But Ellynne was more interested in what made her mother tick. She asked, "Why did you marry Dad?"

Judith looked shocked at the question. "I married your father because he was the best, the kindest, the most wonderful man I'd ever met. He helped me see who I was and what I should be doing with my life. Your father was a wonderful man, Ellynne."

"I've just always wondered. He was a lot older than you."

"He was only fifty when he died," Judith Aleese answered rather sharply.

"I guess your parents didn't approve of the marriage," Ellynne ventured.

Judith Aleese leaned forward and spoke intensely. "Make your own decisions, Ellynne. Live your own life. Don't waste it trying to please other people."

Ellynne realized wryly that her mother was the third person to give her advice tonight. First, Willie told her she mustn't let her beauty turn her into a selfish woman. Then Kip told her about handling obstacles being more important than what happens to you. Now her mother wanted her to lead her own life.

She wondered if anyone would care to give her advice on how to use all that good advice in one evening. Actually, she was feeling tired, sleepy, and relaxed all at once. She yawned and stretched as she said, "I'll try. The dance was fun and Kip asked me out for Saturday night. I had a wonderful time and I think I'll go to sleep."

"But you haven't heard my news," Judith Aleese said. Her eyes were shining. "I did more than apologize to you, you know. I took action. As I was looking in the album, remembering what it was like to be sixteen and shy, Lizzie called."

Ellynne clapped her hand over her mouth. Poor Lizzie! It was the second Friday night in a row when she'd gone out and forgotten to call Lizzie and tell her. Then she felt irritation at Lizzie's faithful keeping of their bargain. The truth was, Ellynne hardly thought about Lizzie at all anymore but Lizzie hung onto the friendship with a fierce grip.

"So I invited Lizzie to come for Easter vacation. She said she could save some spending money by then and I knew you'd have the time free. I'm paying her way as a part of my apology to you. Won't it be wonderful to see her again?" Her mother beamed.

Ellynne could hardly believe what she was hearing. "You invited Lizzie to come here?" she repeated slowly.

"Yes." Judith obviously thought she had just done Ellynne the greatest favor in the world.

Ellynne was almost paralyzed as she realized that Lizzie would absolutely destroy her new image. Lizzie was a nice person, and it was true that they'd been friends since seventh grade, but Lizzie would never, never fit in here. She winced as she remembered Lizzie's coltish, enthusiastic ways. Even though she was almost seventeen, she still seemed to bounce around like a twelve-year-old.

"I don't know," Ellynne said. "I'll be so busy Easter week. I wanted to go to Catalina with a group of kids."

"You can take Lizzie," Judith Aleese said confidently.

"Of course I can," Ellynne said. She hugged her mother and kissed her as she said, "Mom, I think it was great of you to do this for me. You're a wonderful person and I really appreciate it. Of all the parents I know, I would rather have you than any of them. Thanks a lot."

"Wait a minute," Judith said laughingly. "Don't get carried away or I'll think you learned all that applesauce in charm school."

"I really mean it, Mom. You're great."

Judith Aleese kissed her daughter on the cheek and said, "Sleep late tomorrow."

Ellynne nodded her head. No sense telling her mother that she would probably lie awake worrying about how to get out of having Lizzie come visit. She couldn't think of telling her mother that she didn't want her friend. How could she explain that? Her mother would never understand if she said that Lizzie didn't fit into her life anymore.

If she tried to explain to her mother that in Ohio, she and Lizzie had been on the outskirts of the social life — that Lizzie had still never had a date — her mother would have a fit. Things like that didn't matter in Judith Aleese's world, but they mattered a lot in Ellynne's.

Somehow, she had to find some way to keep Lizzie in Ohio where she belonged. There was no way that she was going to tell

Merri that Lizzie was her best friend. Merri would break up with laughter.

As far as that went, she couldn't exactly imagine Lizzie and Willie together either. Willie was so sophisticated in so many ways. She modeled fashions in the Del Amo Mall on Saturdays, dated a college boy, quoted existential philosophers, and she looked like she'd just stepped out of *Seventeen* magazine.

What would Lizzie say to her? Lizzie was so open, so naïve, so simple and childlike, that she might say anything. Ellynne winced as she remembered Lizzie's amazement as she asked, "You mean your best friend out there is *black*?"

No. It wouldn't do at all. Lizzie would be like a fish out of water in Redondo Beach. And Ellynne wasn't going to let loyalty to an old friend ruin her life. In the morning, she would explain this to Judith. After all, her mother was the one who had said, "Live your own life."

Tomorrow, Ellynne thought sleepily as she lay her head on her pillow. She was sure she would find some way to explain it so her mother would understand . . . tomorrow. Then she remembered that Judith would be gone all day.

That was too bad, Ellynne told herself. She would find some way to talk to her mother later in the week. After all, none of the plans were solid yet. There was plenty of time to explain it all to Lizzie and her mother.

Whether she talked with Judith tomorrow or not, it would be a wonderful day, Ellynne thought. She was going to meet Willie for a late lunch and watch the last hour of her modeling job. Then they were coming back here to practice the cheerleading steps.

Willie was just sure Ellynne could be a wonderful cheerleader if she worked harder. Secretly, Ellynne wondered if she would ever get the feel of the handsprings, and she couldn't get over feeling silly, chanting the simple verses while she jumped up and down and yelled. But if the sophisticated Willie could manage it, so could she.

Ellynne's next-to-last thoughts were of Kip smiling down at her as she said, "See you Saturday night." Her last thoughts were of the split she would work on tomorrow afternoon, and her very last thought was, *Maybe something will happen and Lizzie will change her mind about coming.*

Thirteen

The next few weeks seemed to whizz past. There were so many things to do that Ellynne found it very easy to forget her friend Lizzie was still planning to visit at Easter. To tell the truth, she was so busy thinking about Kip Russell and whether or not she could be a cheerleader that she didn't think of Lizzie from one week to the next.

Lizzie called faithfully each Friday night. If Ellynne was out with Kip, she called back on Saturday. Sometimes it was Sunday before they actually talked.

It was on a Sunday afternoon just after New Year's that Lizzie asked her straight out, "Are you sure you want me to come at Easter?"

This was her chance. Lizzie was very sensitive. Ellynne knew she wouldn't really have to say that she didn't want her old friend. All she would have to do was hesitate or beat around the bush. She could just imagine the crushed look on Lizzie's face if she were to say, "Well, I do have a lot of commitments."

Ellynne opened her mouth and what she intended to say just didn't come out. It would hurt too much. Instead, she laughed and said, "Lizzie, what a dumb question! Of course I want you to visit me. We'll have lots of fun. We'll go to Disneyland, to Hollywood, and to the beach. Maybe you'll even meet a movie star."

Lizzie's voice was tight as she pursued it, "Listen, Ellynne, I know you're really popular out there. I wouldn't want to cramp your style."

"This phone call is costing us money so let's not waste it on dumb stuff," Ellynne said lightly. "Anything new in the library?"

"Sort of," Lizzie admitted shyly. "I'm working two nights a week now as well as Saturdays. And Mr. Watson is helping me with my poetry."

"Old Wicked Watson?"

"Yes. He found out about my poems — there were some published in the Sunday magazine — and he liked them. He's spending a lot of time with me, helping me see which ones are good and which are bad." She paused and then she added, "He thinks some are good enough to start sending to literary magazines. He has a friend at *Poets and Pictures* and he's going to help me pick out some to send to him."

That's wonderful, Ellynne thought. She was feeling sort of sick as she imagined Lizzie telling all this to someone like Merri Merriweather. Merri would think writing poetry for a hobby was hysterically funny.

Thinking of Merri reminded her that she had some news for Lizzie. "Kip is taking me skiing tomorrow."

"Skiing? You mean there's snow there?"

"Not in Redondo Beach, silly. It's about seventy degrees today, but we're only two hours from Mt. Baldy. There's snow on Mt. Baldy."

Lizzie thought that was just wonderful. She thought everything Ellynne was doing these days was just wonderful. As Ellynne hung up the phone, she wondered if Lizzie had any idea how much she — Ellynne — had changed this year.

Quickly putting the thought of Easter vacation from her head, Ellynne went into her bedroom and began working out. Each day, she spent a half hour on limbering exercises as well as practicing her jumps and kicks with Willie. Ellynne enjoyed the exercises, especially the yoga stretches, but she wasn't sure she would ever get used to the bouncy jumps and high kicks.

She put on the Fats Waller record that seemed to have the perfect rhythm for her exercises, and began bending and stretching. When the record was over, she played the

Reggae record that Willie had loaned her. The fast, sharp beat seemed to work better for the kicks, handsprings, jumps, and splits she used in her routines.

Exercises over, Ellynne did her homework and then pulled out her secret notebook. Idly, she flipped through the beginning pages, smiling at the promises she'd made herself. Then she entered today's thoughts.

January 5. No school tomorrow. Kip and I are going to Mount Baldy. How I love him. Does he love me? Not yet. He's too involved with studies and work. Is he still dating Merri? Yes. But not as much now. I'm thinking positively about that.

Ellynne turned out the lights and lay down to sleep. She was looking forward so much to this trip tomorrow. Even though Kip always seemed glad to be with her, he still was putting other things first. She was pretty sure he dated her more than Merri and she understood that he had to think about school and jobs, but still she wanted more. *If only Kip would make a commitment*, she thought.

The alarm rang at four and Ellynne was dressed and ready to go by four-thirty when Kip knocked gently on the front door. She carried the plastic shopping bag full of sandwiches and thermos bottles to his car, chatting gaily about the day before them.

Kip drove easily, smiling and answering Ellynne as she asked questions, but apparently content to let her do most of the talking. She told him about her skiing experiences in Ohio, making them sound more glamorous than they really were. Then she told him about her struggles with the handsprings in her cheerleader practice.

"Didn't the records help?" he asked. It had been Kip who suggested she try exercising to music.

"Yes, they helped," she said. "But I wonder if I'll ever really be good. I see some people and they seem to be naturals at it. Willie looks as though she grew up walking the high wire in the circus or something. I just don't have that sort of natural ability."

Ellynne didn't mention Merri by name, but she knew that Merri also had a natural grace and ability that were quite special.

Kip answered slowly, carefully. "Maybe you aren't a natural. But you've been working very hard. Practice and hard work usually pay off, Ellynne. That's one of the things I like about you. You understand the value of work."

Ellynne's stomach did a little flip-flop at the compliment. Maybe Kip's conversation didn't measure up to her dreams but he obviously admired her. She smiled at him and said, "It's nice to be here."

Kip nodded and swung into a Denny's restaurant with a big "Open 24 Hours" sign on the roof. "It will be a lot cheaper to breakfast here than at the Mt. Baldy restaurant," he explained.

Splitting expenses was going to make the trip a bit easier for Kip, but Ellynne realized that he needed to save money for college. She said, "I brought hard-boiled eggs and a thermos of bouillon for breakfast. We can eat in the car."

He smiled down at her and hugged her close to him for a moment before he shook his head. "Got to eat a hearty breakfast, you know. You're in for an athletic day."

Ellynne followed him meekly into the restaurant. Kip seldom touched her and she was still glowing from the hug. If a man hugged you at five-thirty in the morning, then he must care for you — mustn't he?

Kip ate fried eggs, bagels, coffee, and sausage. Ellynne had two scrambled eggs, tea, and one slice of wheat toast. Kip urged her to try the sausage.

She shook her head. By now it had become second nature to ignore people's insistence that she eat more than she needed to. She had a stack of standard responses. This morning she said, "I don't eat much in the morning."

"Or at lunch or dinner," Kip teased. When he saw her face tense, he continued, "But that's O.K. If I wanted a chow hound, I'd ask Lori Smith out."

Ellynne didn't laugh. Lori Smith was a chubby girl in the crowd. Ellynne couldn't even look at her without feeling awful. Each time Lori would come to their table, hoping to be invited to sit down, her tray was loaded with fattening foods. Ellynne always thought, *I used to eat like that. I used to look like that.* And then the fear would strike.

I wonder if I'll ever get over being afraid of food, Ellynne thought. Ever since she'd read that most people who lost weight gained it back within two years and that many fat people who became thin felt fat all the rest of their lives she'd been afraid. Ellynne sighed.

Kip asked, "Such sad thoughts so early in the morning?"

"I was thinking about Lori. She's a nice person but she should lose some weight."

"Lori Smith? She looks all right. Not glamorous like you, but fine."

Ellynne looked at Kip to see if he was kidding. He probably wasn't. Lori Smith was at least as overweight as Ellynne had been before she went on the diet a year and a half ago. Was Kip saying that he thought she would have looked all right then? Ellynne shook her head swiftly and dismissed the thought. Of course Kip wouldn't have been interested in her when she weighed one hundred and forty pounds.

But it was time to climb back into the car and make the slow drive up the mountain road to Mt. Baldy. Traffic was almost bumper-to-bumper for the last twenty minutes up the mountain. As they drove upward, Ellynne

127

was amused at the little dabs of white snow clumped along the edges of the road. What amused her the most was Kip who pointed proudly and said, "See, snow. Just like I promised you."

Ellynne was careful not to sound superior as she said, "It is pretty, isn't it?"

Kip nodded. "I've lived all my life at the beach. It must be very different for you. Do you like it?"

"I like walking on the beach alone on cool days. I liked getting a tan this summer. The beach will be wonderful now that I know so many people."

"It's amazing how popular you've become so quickly," Kip said. "You've only been here three months and you're already thinking of being a cheerleader."

"Not to mention dating the high school football star," Ellynne teased.

Kip put his arm around her shoulder and said, "I'm glad you're here, Ellynne. I'm glad you're in my life."

She leaned her head on his shoulder. "Me too."

They pulled into the parking lot at the foot of Mt. Baldy Ski Resort. Kip turned off the ignition, leaned over, and kissed Ellynne. Ellynne slipped her arms around him and kissed him back. It was their first real kiss and it was wonderful.

It felt good to be in Kip Russell's arms, to be held by him. He was so warm, so gentle, and so strong, all at the same time. As she responded to his kiss, she felt as though she was slipping into a softer, warmer, closer feeling than she'd ever had. *If only it could last forever*, she thought as his arms tightened around her.

Kip drew away from her and looked down at her warm face. He traced one mittened finger down the side of her cheek as he said, "You're quite a girl, Ellynne."

She blushed. Did Kip think she kissed everyone the way she had just kissed him? It would be horrible if he thought that and yet she couldn't help responding to him. She said, "We'd better get going."

Kip laughed and kissed her lightly on the nose. "Yes, Snow Bunny, we'd better stop steaming up the car at seven in the morning."

Ellynne flushed and stepped out of the car. She felt stiff and awkward and awful as she looked around the crowded parking lot of Mt. Baldy Ski Resort. She frowned at herself for being so self-conscious. She'd done nothing wrong, only responded to a kiss and that was normal. If it was natural and normal, why was she so uptight?

Ellynne trudged up the hill toward the beginner's slope in silence as she tried to sort out her feelings. What had happened? She'd kissed Kip Russell and she'd liked it. Nothing wrong there. Then what was wrong?

As they put on their skis and bought tickets for the day's skiing, Ellynne mulled the problem over in her mind. They stood in the long line at the beginner's slope, waiting for the rope tow, and she tried to think of something she could say to break the ice. Kip was talking now, easily and cheerfully, about the surroundings and the ski trails. If he felt awkward, he was covering it well. *He's not worried*, Ellynne thought as she stepped out to catch hold of the rope tow. That's when she understood what was worrying her. It wasn't the way she responded to his kiss at all. She was worrying because he didn't seem to be as involved with her as she was with him.

You can't make him love you, she told herself. *All you can do is hope . . . and give him space to be himself.*

The day was fun but it was soon clear that Kip would never be a skier unless he was willing to put in months of practice. Ellynne showed him the basic steps and he tried gamely, but he fell so often that he finally decided to quit and wait while Ellynne skied.

"I'm holding you up," he protested. "You're a good skier so I'll just be your cheering section. Go on up to the higher slope now. I'll wait down here."

Ellynne wanted to tell him that she would rather be with him than ski, but she didn't want to betray how important it was to her to be beside him. After all, Kip hadn't indicated he wanted to spend the rest of his life with her, only the rest of this day. And he'd spent a lot of his money and time to bring her up here.

Ellynne pointed to the intermediate slope and said, "Watch for me. I'll be wearing a red carnation."

"Sure, Snow Bunny," Kip said and he hugged her again.

Ellynne leaned into him for one brief moment and then went over to catch the chairlift for the intermediate slope. She skied by herself until lunchtime, and then went back to the parking lot to meet Kip as they had arranged.

He was sitting in the car studying his calculus. She leaned against the car window and asked, "Any food left?"

Kip nodded and pointed to a small, sloping hill with picnic tables. "The sun is shining. We could eat over there."

They carried the picnic basket and thermos bottles to the bench and tables. Kip brushed off the light film of snow with his mitten and sat down. "Bet you're used to picnicking in the snow, aren't you?" he asked.

Ellynne smiled at him and shook her head. "Not really. In Ohio it was usually too cold to stay outside except when you were exercising."

"But here you are, picnicking in the snow in sunny California. Watch out you don't get a snowburn. You're very fair." He brushed his snow cap off his head and pulled off his mittens. "It's really warm. Fellow up there said it was forty-five degrees today."

Ellynne bit into an apple. "Must be more than that right now. I'm almost warm." She pulled off her ski jacket and cap.

"You look beautiful, Ellynne. The sunlight is hitting your hair and your face is glowing."

Kip leaned over and held her close. He kissed the top of her head. She leaned her head against his shoulder for a second, smiled up at him, and said, "Sounds like good dialogue from a bad movie."

Kip didn't laugh. He held her close for another moment and then said lightly, "Want to take a walk? I think I'm through skiing today."

Ellynne packed up the lunch, put her hand in Kip's, and they walked up to the top of a hill. Once there, Kip put his arm around her shoulder and said, "If you look straight down that way, you'll see Los Angeles. That is, if you could see past the smog."

"It's beautiful," Ellynne murmured. She hoped that Kip would kiss her again. She hoped that he would ask her to be his girl. But she couldn't tell exactly what he was feeling. Was she just a pretty girl he was dating occasionally? Someone nice to kiss but not to be serious about?

As though he read her thoughts, Kip said, "When I finish college, I'm going to graduate school. It will be eight years before I have my degree. That's a long time away."

Ellynne understood he was telling her he was not in any place to be serious about her or anyone else. She wanted to protest that they didn't have to be *that* serious yet. She wanted to tell him that all she wanted was to be his girl. But Ellynne was wary of pushing Kip, wary of making a fool of herself. She pretended not to understand. She said, "You're lucky. At least you know you're going to be a doctor. I still don't have the foggiest notion what I want to be."

Laughing aloud, she turned to face Kip and said, "This has been a wonderful day." As she said it, she slipped her arms around his neck and stood on her tiptoe so that she could kiss him again.

This time, the kiss lasted longer, was quieter, and less surprising in its intensity. There was a warmth, a friendliness to it that pleased Ellynne very much. As before, she felt she could have stayed there forever, but when Kip drew back, she dropped her arms from his neck quickly.

"Time to start for home," he said quietly. "I have to work this evening."

They talked and laughed a lot on the trip home. Kip entertained Ellynne with tales of his younger brothers' and sisters' antics. When he told her about his sister Betty's boa constrictor, Ellynne said, gasping with laughter, "I don't know whether to envy you or feel sorry for you."

"A bit of both," Kip advised seriously. "It's fun having five brothers and sisters but it can be trouble too. For instance, I'll call you later in the week. I'm not sure I can ask you out next weekend. I may have to babysit with my sister while the rest of the family goes to San Francisco."

Ellynne kissed him lightly on the cheek as she unlocked the car door. "I'll see you at school tomorrow. Thanks again for a wonderful day."

She watched Kip drive away from the house with mixed feelings that included worry that she'd seemed too eager, delight that he'd finally kissed her and seemed to like it, disappointment that he hadn't asked her to be his steady girl, amusement that he had to apologize in advance for not asking her out next weekend, and most of all — joy in remembering the thrill of being held close and kissed by Kip Russell.

It *had* been a wonderful day.

Fourteen

During the next few weeks, Ellynne saw Kip often, but she couldn't help knowing he was also dating Merri. At first, she hoped he was just being nice and would let Merri go gently. When Merri made a point of telling Ellynne that Kip invited her to be his date on his birthday, she had to recognize the truth.

"He's just not ready to settle down," Willie said. "You've got to give him a chance to make up his own mind."

Ellynne kicked high as she kept time to the music, then jumped into a wide-legged stance and bent her head down. As Willie urged her, "Lower, lower," Ellynne groaned and shook her head.

"If it were any other girl," Ellynne complained. "But what does he want Merri for? She's so snide about it."

"Bend deeper from the waist. You look like a fifty-year-old woman with arthritis. Merri is . . . Merri is Merri. A bit of a snob but talented. You've got to admit she's cute. Not classy like you, but cute."

"He invited her out on his birthday. It must be that he likes her best." Ellynne bent deeper and deeper. Groaning, she continued, "I would have baked him a cake. Chocolate with frosting."

Willie laughed. "Maybe you should have told him that. Maybe he was afraid you'd try to frost it with yogurt and wheat germ or something."

Ellynne stopped the tape and flopped onto the bed. "I quit. I'm tired." She lay out straight and put her hands under her head. Staring at the ceiling she said, "She's going to beat me, isn't she?"

"With Kip or cheerleading?"

"Both." Ellynne couldn't keep the self-pity out of her voice. "I've worked so hard and Merri is going to beat me in the long run. She's got natural talent and all I've got . . ."

"All you've got is a bad case of the blues," Willie said as she tossed a stuffed animal at Ellynne's head. "It's a big world out there. There's more competition in this world than Merri Merriweather, you know. You're going to be one of those classy dames who is always miserable because there are other classy-looking dames?"

"Willie, you know I'm not like that. You're the best-looking girl in the school and I'm not jealous of you. It's just Merri is always so cutsie when Kip is around and so nasty when he isn't. I hate to see her beat me. Besides, I . . . I don't understand how Kip can . . ."

Willie laughed, "How Kip can be so sweet on you one night and out with that one the next? Life's tough." She dropped her teasing tone and said seriously, "I think Merri will probably get a place as a cheerleader. She almost made it last year and she's probably better this year. But there are three places. You, me, and Merri. That's what we need to aim for."

"That's a team."

"We'll have her outnumbered," Willie said. "As for your boy, I suppose he thinks Merri is cute. I suppose he thinks you're too good to be true. I suppose he's playing the field so he can keep things under control. That's what I suppose. But if I were you, I'd ask him."

"Maybe I'll do that," Ellynne said thoughtfully. "Maybe I'll try and talk with him."

But in spite of what she'd said to Willie, when the time came, she was the one who didn't want to talk about Merri. She and Kip were sitting in her living room, listening to a new Ida Mae Cox record. Kip said, "Tomorrow is my birthday and I've invited Merri to go into Hollywood to see a show."

"That's nice," Ellynne said. She offered him the bowl of popcorn.

"I'd like to try and explain . . ."

"There's nothing to explain," Ellynne said sharply. "After all, we're not going steady. I mean, we're really just good friends, not lovers."

Kip looked startled. "Certainly not lovers but surely more than friends?"

Ellynne jumped up and ran over to the stack of records to find a livelier one. She said, "There's nothing to explain so let's change the subject. How's your new position as assistant to the assistant manager going?"

Kip was now serving as general assistant and check casher for his supermarket. "They offered me a part-time job while I'm in college. They'll let me work out my own schedule."

"Oh, Kip, that's wonderful," Ellynne said. She was truly delighted for him. She was also very glad to think that he might be staying in Redondo Beach instead of going away to school.

"I don't know," Kip said. "I still think I may get a scholarship that will be big enough to let me live on campus. I'd love to go to Berkeley or Santa Cruz."

"But if you were here, you could watch me at the games," Ellynne said. "At least, I hope you could watch me. The first elimination trials are next week."

"You'll make it," Kip said confidently. "You've worked so hard." He laughed. "If we'd had you on the football team, we might not have lost all the games. We needed some people with perseverance."

Ellynne stood up, holding the Billie Holiday record she'd been looking for. "Speaking of perseverance, will you help me with my science before you leave?"

They spent the next hour sitting on the couch, working on science, eating popcorn, and listening to Billie Holiday. As Kip left, he kissed her good-night and said, "It was another wonderful evening with my wonderful girl."

"Happy birthday," Ellynne whispered, but she did not give him the silver chain with the tiny elephant charm she'd chosen for him. How could she give a birthday present to a fellow who was taking another girl out on his birthday?

The minute Kip left the room, Ellynne burst into tears and ran sobbing to her room. When her mother came in at midnight, she was still sobbing. Judith Aleese knocked on the door and asked, "Are you all right?"

"I have a cold," Ellynne answered. In the old days, when she was younger, she could have gone to her mother for advice, but not tonight. Tonight she was in no mood for Judith Aleese's cheerful insistence that there were more important things in life than boys. Ellynne stopped crying and willed herself to sleep. After all, it would be horrible if she looked tired and ugly tomorrow. She couldn't think of anything more terrible than letting Merri Merriweather know how much she cared.

Ellynne became quite good at looking as though she didn't care the next few days. Merri raved about the wonderful time she and Kip had in Hollywood as though it had been a trip to the moon. It seemed to Ellynne that no matter what the subject was, Merri managed to turn it to that fabulous evening.

On Thursday, the day before the tryouts for cheerleader finalists, Willie said at lunch, "This chop suey looks to me like chops that should be sued."

"Kip suggested Chinese food . . ." Merri began.

"Can it," Willie interrupted. "We all know that you had Greek food. We know how the grape leaves were rolled, how the hamburger was cooked, and that he brought you one single rose. What we don't know . . . what we don't know is why he invited you."

Merri's eyes blazed as she retorted, "You don't need to be rude to me, Willie. Just because you're a cheerleader, you don't need to think that I'll let you get away with being rude to me."

"I don't mean to be rude," Willie said good-naturedly. "But you won't take a hint. I'm tired of hearing about your date with Kip Russell."

"You're just mad because he didn't ask your friend, there." Merri pointed a fork at

Ellynne and managed to sound slightly threatening as she said, "Maybe he'll never ask your friend out again."

Ellynne's face flushed and she felt like she would like to run away from the table. She felt like an absolute fool to be involved in a silly quarrel over a boy. As a matter of fact, Kip had asked her out for Friday night and she'd turned him down. She wanted to practice her cheers that night so she would be absolutely in top form on Saturday morning for the tryouts.

But under no circumstances would Ellynne have told Merri a thing about her relationship with Kip Russell. It was Willie who pointed her fork back at Merri and said, "It so happens that Kip has already asked Ellynne out."

"That's because I was busy," Merri answered promptly.

Ellynne winced. She wondered if that was true as she said, "Please . . ."

"You listen, Merri. There's a very good chance we'll be cheering together next year, and if you're going to be on our team, you're going to have to learn to behave."

"You and I will be cheerleaders," Merri said. "She won't. She's too shy. I've seen her and she'll never make it."

Ellynne could stand no more. She rose, said, "I've got to get to science. See you tomorrow," and left the cafeteria.

That afternoon, she tried to explain to Willie, "I just felt awful, having you defend me like that."

"It's a good thing I did," Willie grumbled. "You certainly can't defend yourself. Why did you let her get away with that?"

"Maybe Merri's right," Ellynne said. "Maybe I am too shy. Too stiff. What if I don't make it?"

"Relax. You know you'll be one of the ten finalists. Then we'll work some more on that handspring and jump. You've just got to get over your self-consciousness, you know."

"Let's work right now," Ellynne said. She put on her favorite record and went through her routines one more time. At five, when her mother came in, Judith Aleese shook her head and said, "If you spent half as much time on science as you did on cheers, you'd have the Nobel Prize by now."

"Tryouts tomorrow morning," Ellynne answered as she worked her way through the front handspring. "Wish me luck." Judith Aleese watched her daughter quietly for a moment and then said in a sad voice, "I wish you the very best this world has to offer, Ellie. You've got beauty, brains, and health. You don't need luck."

"I need luck," Ellynne grumbled under her breath. She was standing on her head, trying to improve her balance.

Thirty-two girls lined up the next afternoon, and half of them were eliminated almost immediately. Ellynne didn't blame the coach, but she was sorry for the sixteen girls who were so quickly brushed aside.

That left sixteen young women competing for ten finalist spots. The ten would have all of March and most of April to learn the cheers and steps. Then on the Tuesday after Easter vacation, two girls would be selected as cheerleaders for the next school year. Willie already had the third spot.

First the girls performed in a line step.

They went through some simple march steps and side bends and clapping routines so that the coach could get an idea of their ability to stay in step and whether or not they had any rhythm.

Willie squeezed her hand as Ellynne stepped out of line to perform her solo cheer. She took a deep breath, jumped high in the air, and then jumped three more times, ending with a side arch. She then went into a simple cheer, moving through the leans, bends, and arm motions with ease. The cheer ended with another high jump and then a circular motion of the arms. As she moved she chanted:

Good, better, best,
We'll put them to the test.
'Cause good we are
And better we'll be,
We're the best!
Yes sir-ree!

It was the cheer she'd done at her birthday party, and she started with it for good luck. Without pausing, she took a deep breath and moved into a more complicated routine. In this one, she used stomping and hand-clapping until the end when she had to jump in the air and do a Herkie, which was sort of a split.

Hee'y . . . Clap your hands.
(*stomp-clap, stomp-clap-clap*)
(*stomp-clap, stomp-clap-clap*)
Hey all you Tiger fans,
Stand up and clap your hands.
(*stomp-clap, stomp-clap-clap*)
(*stomp-clap, stomp-clap-clap*)
Hey, now get in the beat,
Stand up and move your feet.
(*stomp-clap, stomp-clap-clap*)
(*stomp-clap, stomp-clap-clap*)
Hey now get in the groove,
This time let's really move.
(*stomp-clap, stomp-clap-clap*)
(*stomp-clap, stomp-clap-clap*)
(*stomp-clap, stomp-clap-clap*)
Let's move!

She was ready to move into a third cheer that would include a handspring, but the coach motioned her to stop. That was fine because she still looked awkward and stiff on the handspring and back bends. There was no doubt that some of the other girls had

144

more natural agility than she did, but Ellynne wasn't surprised when she was chosen one of the ten finalists. She was clearly better than most of them and she was surer of her cheers. What worried her was that after she saw Merri in action, she realized that there were really eight girls competing for one spot. Merri was already almost as good as Willie, and Ellynne knew she hadn't even started practicing.

Ellynne hadn't been surprised at how good Merri was — she'd been warned of that. What surprised her was how good several of the other girls were. A slim redhead named Katherine Kelly bounced up and down with the alacrity of a firecracker. As the cheer music started, Katherine changed from a frail and gentle Renaissance maiden into a fountain of cheerful energy and optimism. *She's got pep*, Ellynne thought sadly.

But Katherine wasn't the only excellent competitor. Marsha Browing was a short, enthusiastic black girl with an entirely different style from Willie. She cracked jokes and bent her body as though it were silly putty. Marsha, though lacking grace, was really awfully good.

So was Virginia Hanson. In fact, Virginia was almost as good as Merri and very similar in style. Merri had the ability to move quickly to the music and seem relaxed and effortless while she did it. If anything, Virginia had more grace than any of them. She bent and twisted and flowed like a Chinese willow tree.

Ellynne hated to admit to herself that any of the other three girls were in the running. And the worst of it was that each of them would complement Merri and Willie nicely. In their initial planning, Willie had promised, "The judges will have to pick you, Ellynne. You would look so good in the middle, between Merri and me."

They had imagined Willie, tall and brown and slim, on one side, and Merri, short and curly-haired and cute on the other. "You'd be perfect in the middle with your blonde class," Willie said.

Ellynne closed her eyes and imagined each of the competitors in that middle spot. Virginia Hanson, with her graceful style would offer essentially the same characteristics and contrasts that she — Ellynne — offered. Marsha, with her jazzy style and bouncy energy, would add an enthusiasm that the judges might find irresistible. And Katherine Kelly would add red hair, gentle looks, and cheerful optimism to the team.

I'm glad I don't have to choose, Ellynne thought. *They all looked wonderful.*

Merri seemed delighted as she asked in the girl's locker room after practice, "Wasn't Virginia wonderful?"

Willie nodded. "So was Ellynne."

"And Marsha and Katherine," Ellynne added.

Merri seemed convinced that Virginia was the leading contender and immediately went over to talk with her, offering to help her practice the steps. Virginia flushed rosy red and shyly accepted the offer.

On the way out of the gym, Ellynne said, "Merri is going to help Virginia and you're going to help me. This is turning into a real battle."

Willie growled, "There's some stiff competition there. And honey, this is no battle, this is war!"

Fifteen

Ellynne practiced so much the next four weeks that she dreamed of cheers. Those weren't bad dreams though. The bad dreams were when she dreamed of losing.

One night, she woke in a sweat, to find Judith Aleese beside her. Her mother said, "You were calling out in your sleep." She sat on the edge of her daughter's bed and brushed the hair back from her face as she asked, "Ellie, what's wrong?"

"Nothing, Mom. Just a nightmare, I guess."

"Ellie, is it you and Kip? Is something . . . troubling you? Do you think you're too serious about him?"

Ellynne smiled wryly and answered, "No need to worry about that, Mom. Kip and I aren't serious about each other. I see him once a week — or once every other week — but he's still dating Merri." She added despondently, "Yesterday, I heard he took Lori Smith to the movies." Bitterness washed over her as she thought of how hard she'd worked to become a slim and glamorous 110 pounds. Now Kip was dating a girl who must weigh close to Ellynne's original weight!

"Ellie," her mother said gently, "perhaps Kip is wise not to get too involved with one girl at this time in his life."

"Oh, Mother," Ellynne said in exasperation, "I'm not asking Kip to marry me. But why can't he see how much I. . . ." Her voice trailed off. She didn't want to use the word *love*. It would kill her if her mother laughed at her.

"How much you love him?" Judith Aleese added gently. She shook her head. "We don't always get what we want, Ellie. Maybe you've got to work on loving Kip enough to let him choose his own way. Maybe you're really more interested in making *him* love you than in loving him."

Ellynne nodded her head and said, "I think I'm sleepy." She didn't want to quarrel with her mother and she didn't want to listen to a lecture. Judith Aleese sighed, then patted her hand, and went to her own room. Ellynne entertained herself with a dream of how wonderful it would be when she became a cheerleader and Kip saw her with new eyes.

In her dream, she had him saying, "You looked lovely, Ellynne. You looked beautiful." She remembered that wonderful day at Mt. Baldy when he had actually told her how beautiful she was. She put herself to sleep, imagining she was in Kip's arms, being held as he had held her that magical day.

But it wasn't only Kip that was worrying Ellynne. It was also the cheerleader competition. She and Willie were working out every afternoon after school. Ellynne was trying to change her style to a peppier one. She was convinced that her only hope of winning the third spot was to develop a more enthusiastic delivery.

"I want to jump as high as Katherine with as much enthusiasm as Marsha and as much grace as Virginia," she said. "I want it all."

She was working out with the gym coach on Tuesdays and Thursdays now, as well as with Willie. So were the other girls. In a way, Ellynne wished she didn't have to work out with her competition. Each time she saw Virginia Hanson, she got nervous. Virginia seemed to get better and better each day while Ellynne knew she was definitely on a plateau.

Tuesday afternoon, the coach put on "Stars and Stripes Forever" and started to instruct. She asked, "Where are Sally and Hortensia?"

"They dropped out," Merri volunteered with glee. "Hortensia said the competition was too stiff."

Coach Barnes merely nodded. And the girls began to run through their steps.

Now we are six, Ellynne thought. Merri was so much better than the others that she didn't think of her as being in the competition. Then for one moment she thought, *What if I made it and Merri didn't?* Ellynne shook her head as she lost her step in the line. That could simply never happen. Merri had natural talent and she was working hard. Ellynne was working harder but she still felt stiff and uncomfortable much of the time.

"You're out of step," Coach Barnes warned. That was when it happened.

The line was getting ready for a series of jumps and on the first jump, Virginia Hanson came crashing to the floor. She screamed out in pain.

Coach Barnes ran to her and the other girls stopped jumping. Girls had fallen before, but everyone immediately knew this was no ordinary fall. Virginia looked down at her ankle and cried, "It's broken. It's broken."

After that, everything happened quickly. One of the other coaches came running and they carried Virginia to the office on a stretcher.

The girls stood around in little clusters, talking of the suddenness of the accident. It was Marsha who said what they were all thinking. "If Virginia's ankle is really broken, she's out of the competition."

Coach Barnes was back in a few minutes, dismissing the group, and she said, "Virginia's ankle is broken. I'm going to the hospital with her. See you Thursday."

The girls broke up quickly, each going her

own way, without talking much. Ellynne went right home, worked on her science, started supper, and was waiting for her mother when she came in.

"Virginia Hanson broke her ankle today," Ellynne said.

"You sound glad," Judith Aleese said.

Ellynne shrugged. "It's only an ankle. Am I supposed to cry?"

Judith's eyes narrowed and she said, "That settles it. I'm taking you out of that cheerleader thing."

"Because someone broke her ankle?" Ellynne asked in amazement.

"No. Because it's turning you into a monster. You're actually glad that poor girl broke her ankle."

"I'm not glad. I never said I was glad. You're making a big deal out of nothing."

"You're coming off the team," Judith said fiercely. "I've waited long enough for you to come to your senses."

"Come to my senses? I've worked so hard all year . . ."

"Yes," her mother interrupted. "You've worked hard all year but for all the wrong things. All you ever think about is boys and popularity and clothes and cheerleading. I didn't move to Southern California so you could turn into a mindless teeny-bopper."

"You've been mad ever since we came here. You wanted me to be miserable. You wanted me to be fat. You wanted me not to be popular. That's why you invited Lizzie here for Easter. You're trying to sabotage everything I've worked for!"

"Lizzie?" Judith said. "What has Lizzie got to do with this? She's your friend."

"She's going to spoil my chances for cheerleader," Ellynne sobbed, hating herself as she spoke. "But I don't care what you say, I'm not dropping out of the competition. I've worked too hard. I'm going to try out."

Judith Aleese collapsed in front of her daughter's determination.

"I guess you're right. You have worked hard. And you have got a right to make your own mistakes. But, Ellie, try and listen to me . . . nothing is worth making yourself this miserable for. And nothing is worth turning yourself into a miserable person about."

But Ellynne was trying not to listen. She was just standing politely, with tears streaming down her face until her mother finished.

Sixteen

Ellynne and Willie went to visit Virginia. The gentle, red-haired girl seemed genuinely glad to see them. She said, "I'll be on this couch for two more weeks. My ankle wasn't broken, it was shattered."

"I'll never understand how you did it," Willie said. "You really crashed."

Virginia laughed and reached for a chocolate candy. "It's a break for me in more than one way. Now I have an excuse to quit cheerleader practice and read books while I eat candy. In my secret heart, I'm a softie — a girl who would rather lie in bed with a good book than bounce around in the air."

Ellynne admired Virginia's ease in accepting her disappointment. *Could I do that*? she wondered. Suddenly, she remembered the first time she'd danced with Kip. What was it he had said?

"A friend told me once, 'You become what you are because of the way you handle the obstacles you meet,'" Ellynne offered shyly. "You seem to be becoming a real winner lying there eating candy and reading books."

Virginia smiled gratefully at Ellynne. She said, "You'll be a good cheerleader, Ellynne."

Ellynne blushed. With Virginia in bed with a fractured ankle and the competition only twelve days away, it was clear that she had a better chance. She said, "You may not believe this, but I'm really sorry you broke your ankle."

"I believe it," Virginia answered simply and Ellynne felt a lot better than she had since she'd quarrelled with her mother. After all, it was true. She hadn't wished any harm to Virginia. Nor had she done anything to hurt her. Still, she was glad that Virginia was the sort of person she was. *If that had been Merri,* Ellynne thought, but then she didn't finish the thought because Willie and Virginia were talking.

"So it really wasn't my fault that I found out who they were — I just did," Virginia said. Her eyes were twinkling as she added, "Of course, I didn't tell anyone until today."

"Have you any idea whether Merri told anyone else?" Willie asked.

Virginia shook her head. "Merri wouldn't. She . . . she doesn't really like any of the other girls." She turned to Ellynne and said simply, "I'm sorry I haven't been friendlier to you. I know you're new to the school and all. I'm sorry if I was stand-offish."

Ellynne shook her head in a fast, quick denial. They both knew that Virginia was offering apologies for believing Merri's opinion of Ellynne.

Willie cut back to the main subject. "So you're sure they're the judges — Coach Baker from the high school and Lydia Langtree?" Lydia Langtree was the owner of an expensive specialty shop in the shopping plaza. She'd been so successful she had a chain of six other stores.

Virginia nodded. "I'm sure. I've known for two weeks. Merri's mother golfs with Lydia Langtree every Monday."

"Conflict of interest," Willie growled.

Ellynne laughed. "We'd better not count on getting my mother on the case. She hopes I lose."

Suddenly, Willie looked worried. "I turned down a modeling job at Lydia Langtree's. You don't suppose she holds grudges."

Both Virginia and Ellynne declared in one breath, "She wouldn't dare."

"Lydia Langtree is Bruce Davidson's aunt," Ellynne offered timidly. "When Bruce took me to the Homecoming Dance, he told me."

"And she's crazy about horses and golf," Virginia said. "Merri caddied for her mother and Lydia the last two Saturdays." The twinkle returned to her eyes, "Unfortunately, Merri is scared of horses so she had to turn down a trip to the stables."

Ellynne felt sorry for Virginia and for perhaps the thousandth time, thanked her lucky stars that she'd run into Willie Evans the first day of school. Willie had been a very good friend and good friends were important.

The thought of friends reminded her that Lizzie would be arriving in three days. A sinking feeling hit the pit of her stomach. She decided to ask Willie's advice about how to handle Lizzie's visit as they left Virginia's house.

But Willie was full of plans about how to "psych" Bruce's aunt. She said, "The minute you get home, you call Bruce Davidson on the telephone and ask him to come over and help you . . . what's he good at?"

"Science. Everyone's better at science than I am."

"Ask him to help you with science. Then ask him to the movies. Then ask him to put in a good word for you with his aunt."

"That's cheating!"

"That's *not* cheating. That's using the old bean. How many times have I told you you've got to decide what you want and go after it?"

"I wish you were going to be here next week. Easter vacation will be funny without you."

"I've decided what I want and I'm going after it," Willie said teasingly. She was flying to Berkeley to spend the week with her boyfriend. "Just remember, no matter what happens, you can handle it if you stay goal-oriented."

Ellynne said, "You make everything seem so simple. I wish I had a psychiatrist for a father."

"You don't think I learned these things from him? Absolutely not! All he knows is deep, dark, dreadful things like compulsions and anxieties. I get the good stuff from my mother. She's into positive thinking."

"So is my mother," Ellynne said. "But right now, I'm not sure she's thinking very positively about me. We had a fight. She thinks I'm turning into a monster."

Willie looked her over speculatively and shook her head. "Not really. Your claws are slightly green and your gills are growing a bit larger. The spines on the back of your neck bristle in the breeze, but except for that you're still plain old ordinary Ellynne that everyone knows and loves."

Willie left her laughing, but she was still worried. What good was it going to do to invite Bruce to the movies if Lizzie spoiled everything next week? She winced as she imagined Lizzie bouncing into the soda shop, trilling in her exuberant voice, "Oh look, they've got Ginsberg. I just love Ginsberg's poems!"

No. It wouldn't do. She wasn't going to take Lizzie to the soda shop. She wasn't going to take her to the beach where all the kids from school went. She wasn't going to take her miniature golfing or dancing at the disco. She would have to take her onto the Redondo pier because Lizzie would figure out something was wrong if she didn't, but she wasn't going to introduce her old friend to *any* of the kids at school.

Bruce was delighted to offer her help with her homework, and he promised he'd be over within an hour. Ellynne felt kind of foolish encouraging Bruce after all these months, but she went right ahead and asked him to go to the movies Saturday night.

"Gee, I'd love to, but I'm leaving for Catalina Saturday at noon. Aren't you going over?"

Ellynne shook her head quickly. "I can't. An old friend is coming to town. I'll be showing her around."

"Show her Catalina," Bruce said. "A lot of kids are going over on Saturday and spending the week. I'm only staying two days."

"Will you go over this theory with me one more time?" Ellynne asked to change the subject. "I just don't think I'll ever understand it."

Kip called while Bruce was there, and Ellynne felt funny talking with him while Bruce sat in her living room, reading her term paper. Though Kip dated other girls, Ellynne hadn't really been out with any other fellows. The main reason she felt disloyal was that Kip was the one who had helped her write that paper.

"I've got the evening off," Kip said. "Want to come over and listen to records?"

"I can't," Ellynne answered. "Bruce Davidson is here helping me with my science paper." She expected Kip to make some sort of joking answer.

"Oh," he said. His voice was flat and kind of funny as he said, "Well, I'll call you later."

When Ellynne hung up the telephone, her hand was shaking. Would she ever hear from Kip again? It was silly to feel so threatened, but she was still crazy about him. Kip was the fellow she wanted to be with, but it was Bruce who was sitting in her living room.

Bruce offered a couple of suggestions on the science paper and Ellynne made him two corned beef sandwiches and a Coke. As he tuned in the local rock and roll station, Ellynne wondered, *Did Kip call Merri when he hung up?*

That thought spurred her into saying softly to Bruce, "I'm so worried about the cheerleader contest. I do hope I make it."

Bruce answered, "I told my aunt that you were a special friend. I also let her know you were my pick. She'll probably fool herself into thinking my opinion doesn't matter, but I think it does. After all, I'm her only nephew." He bit into one of the sandwiches. "Good corned beef."

"Thank you, Bruce," Ellynne said simply. She felt rather foolish luring Bruce into her living room and turning on the charm when it really wasn't necessary. Bruce was a nice fellow and she should have known he would do what he could for her. She couldn't help wondering again if the things her mother had said to her could be true.

At seven, Ellynne walked down to the corner to pick up a newspaper for her mother. Bruce waited in the apartment, watching a batch of cookies in the oven. When Ellynne came back, Bruce was talking on the telephone.

He was laughing and said in a teasing voice, "Here she is now, but I'm not sure if I'll let you talk to her."

Ellynne wondered if it was Kip on the line. No. Bruce wouldn't use that teasing tone with Kip. She took the phone from him and said warily, "Hello."

"Hi." It was Lizzie.

"Is that a new fellow?" Lizzie asked. "He sounds darling."

Ellynne looked at Bruce who was pulling the cookies out of the oven. He was tall, slim, sort of good-looking, with a straight, rather prominent nose and high cheekbones. Funny she'd never thought about it before, but Bruce Davidson was probably one of the handsomest boys in school. "Yes," Ellynne said speculatively, "I think he is."

"You're so lucky," Lizzie said with no envy

in her voice. "I can hardly wait to get there. Oh, Ellie, won't we have fun?"

Ellynne's voice was bright but her heart was dull as she answered, "Sure we will."

"Bruce invited me to Catalina. Do you think we could go?"

"Too expensive," Ellynne said shortly. "But we can go to Hollywood, Disneyland, and Knott's Berry Farm."

The girls chatted a few more minutes. Then Lizzie said, "So I'll see you on Saturday morning. That's tomorrow — sort of."

Ellynne agreed. "Five in the morning might just as well be Friday night. But I'll be there."

"Let me say good-bye to her," Bruce insisted.

Ellynne was a bit surprised but she handed the telephone to Bruce. He chatted lightly with Lizzie for a few minutes, then hung up. He asked, "Is your friend as nice as she sounds?"

Ellynne didn't know what to answer. If she sounded too enthusiastic, Bruce might want to meet her. Under no circumstances was she going to introduce Lizzie to Bruce Davidson a week before the cheerleading contest. Finally, she settled for a dazzling smile and a teasing, "How can you think of other women when I'm such a good cook?" She offered him a cookie and motioned for him to come back to the living room.

Bruce Davidson kissed her good-night. She was pleasantly surprised to discover that she liked being kissed by Bruce, though it didn't feel as thrilling as when she was with Kip.

He said, "Thanks for a good evening, Ellynne. I'll call you when I get back from Catalina, and remember, you and Lizzie are coming to my beach party."

"If we can!" Ellynne answered, but she was going to do everything she could to keep him from meeting Lizzie. What would a fellow with an aunt who ran the fanciest women's store in town think about frumpy Lizzie with her plaid skirts and fuzzy ankle socks?

"And I'll mention your name to Lydia again and again," he promised.

When Ellynne wrote about the evening in her secret notebook, she discovered that she had so many feelings it was hard to even determine if it was a good or bad evening. Finally, she drew a line and put things under two headings. On the plus side, she listed Bruce's help with his aunt, his pleasant manner, and his approval of her research paper. On the minus side, she listed his phone talk with Lizzie and Kip's call. For a moment or two, she wondered where to put the kiss. She decided that the best thing of all would be to ignore it.

Seventeen

On the way to the airport, Judith Aleese said, "Ellie, I want you to remember your manners while Lizzie is here. It may be I made a mistake inviting her, but that's not Lizzie's fault. You are not to embarrass me or yourself."

Ellynne stared out the window at the small houses on either side of the street. At four-thirty in the morning, California looked like a black and white set for a bad movie.

"Did you hear me?" her mother insisted.

"Yes. I'll mind my manners."

They said nothing else to each other until they saw the passengers walking down the long tunnel at the arrival terminal. Judith Aleese grabbed Ellynne's arm and said, "There she is. She must be early."

Ellynne couldn't see anyone who looked like Lizzie until she was about ten feet from her. She had time to think, *But she's had her hair cut*, and then Lizzie was hugging her fiercely. Lizzie was so enthusiastic that Ellynne was afraid she might knock her down.

She talked a mile a minute, punctuating her monologue with little squeals of delight. "It's just like a dream," she said over and over. And she insisted on making herself the center of a little mock drama. "Imagine me, Lizzie Lawrence, here in Hollywood!"

Judith Aleese took them to breakfast at the airport restaurant. Lizzie chattered and was so happy that she reminded Ellynne of a six-year-old child. At one point, she actually got up on her knees in the booth and pointed out the window at a landing plane. Ellynne blushed. What if Lizzie acted like that around Merri or Kip? She would just die of shame.

As they were waiting in the cashier's line to pay the bill, Lizzie repeated, "Imagine me, Lizzie Lawrence, here in Hollywood. I hope I see a movie star!"

An older couple turned and smiled at the girls and again, Ellynne blushed scarlet. She snapped at Lizzie, "You're repeating yourself."

Lizzie's face collapsed in surprise and hurt. She nodded and agreed, "I guess I am."

It was Judith who did most of the talking on the way home, telling Lizzie about her progress in law school, about Southern California, and about Ellynne's success at school. Ellynne thought she detected just a faint tinge of pride in her mother's voice as she said, "And now she's trying out to be a cheerleader."

Lizzie turned and looked at Ellynne. She said quietly, "You didn't tell me that."

"I would have told you if I won," Ellynne answered simply. She didn't tell Lizzie that she wanted to be a cheerleader so much she was afraid to discuss it with her old friend. Somehow, talking to Lizzie about it might have made the whole project seem absolutely impossible.

Just being with Lizzie was bringing back all the old feelings of shyness and ordinariness that she used to feel. Lizzie looked a lot better now that she was wearing horn-rimmed glasses and had her hair cropped close and shaped, but she was still the same old Lizzie. *I'll bet she still hasn't had a date*, Ellynne thought, and she couldn't help feeling as though she were a lot older and smarter than her friend.

When they got home, Lizzie asked, "What are we going to do today?"

"You're going to take a nap," Judith said jokingly. "Later, I suppose Ellynne will want to take you down to the beach and maybe introduce you to some friends."

"Not many people in town," Ellynne said quickly. "Willie went to San Francisco to visit her boyfriend."

Judith looked suspiciously at her daughter but said nothing. Ellynne suggested, "We could take the bus into Hollywood this afternoon and walk around. You could pick us up at dinner time and we could see a show."

"That's fine," Judith said quickly. "I've resigned myself to playing chauffeur this week."

"I'll take us all to dinner," Lizzie offered. "And I have a wonderful surprise. Uncle Ben gave me money to take us to Catalina."

"Isn't that wonderful!!" Judith Aleese said.

"Just wonderful," Ellynne agreed but her heart was not in it. It was going to be really tough avoiding anyone from school on Catalina Island. From what she'd heard, there was only one beach and that was only a block wide. Still, there was no way she could get out of accepting the invitation since Lizzie knew all about the island. Ellynne wished that Bruce hadn't been so friendly on the telephone. As she wished it, she cancelled her negative thoughts by reminding herself that she was committed to seeing that Lizzie had a good time. Whatever happened, she would get through it.

They flew to Catalina on Monday and within thirty minutes after their plane skimmed to a stop on the water, they ran into someone from Redondo High. Ellynne and Lizzie checked into the Catalina Motel, and while they were in the lobby, a sophomore Ellynne knew only by sight said, "Hi, Ellynne, did you just get here?"

"Yes." She introduced Lizzie and then added, "I don't know your name, I'm sorry."

The girl supplied her name and offered a fast tour of the island. "Of course you'll have to rent bikes and see the bird sanctuary and tonight you can go dancing at the Casino. But mostly, there's the beach." She laughed and said, "It looks like an extension of Redondo High today. There must be about fifty kids there."

Ellynne's heart sank. Bruce would be there and that was that. She wondered who else she might meet. And how would Lizzie fit in? Not very well, was her guess. Beside Lizzie, this freshman girl seemed positively ancient. Lizzie was looking at the postcards now, squealing in that delighted little voice about the beauties of Catalina Island.

As they carried their bags into the motel room, Lizzie said, "Isn't this wonderful? I never thought I'd get here. Imagine me, Lizzie Lawrence of Ohio, in a glamorous place like Catalina Island."

"You make Ohio sound as if it's a hillbilly town or something," Ellynne snapped.

Lizzie said nothing as she unpacked her small bag and pulled out the bikini she would wear to the beach. When Ellynne asked, "Do you want to go to the bird sanctuary first or the beach?"

"It's up to you, Ellie," Lizzie said meekly.

"And don't call me Ellie!"

There were tears in Lizzie's eyes as she said, "I'm sorry. I don't mean to but I just forget. It's so wonderful being here and I'm so excited that I forget. I'm sorry . . ." she trailed off.

Ellynne felt like a monster. Feeling like a monster made her crosser and grumpier than ever. She said, "Let's take a swim and then have lunch. We can rent bikes and go up to the bird sanctuary later."

"That's fine," Lizzie agreed quickly.

The girls walked through the street past the shops full of tourist souvenirs, the restaurants, and the arcades full of pinball machines. Everywhere they looked, young people on bicycles whizzed by them. Everyone looked as if having a good time was the most important thing in the world. The more the sun shone, the happier everyone else looked, and the worse Ellynne felt.

It didn't cheer her up to hear someone calling, "Ellynne! Ellynne Aleese!"

Ellynne's heart sank but there was nothing she could do except turn to face Bruce Davidson. Bruce was holding two ice cream cones that were melting all over his hands. He said, "I'll bet you're Lizzie. I'm Bruce. We talked on the phone."

Lizzie smiled and said, "I would have known you anywhere."

For the life of her, Ellynne couldn't see what was funny about that, but Bruce laughed and laughed. Lizzie added, "I just think it's wonderful that we ended up over here in Catalina the way you suggested. Imagine me, Lizzie Lawrence from Ohio, all the way in Catalina Island! I just can't get over it."

Ellynne waited with a sinking heart for Bruce to decide that Lizzie was silly and juvenile and walk away. Bruce Davidson might be a little out of touch as Merri had said, but he was one of the most sophisticated kids in school. He lived in a big house right on the beach and traveled a lot with his father, who had something to do with movies.

Bruce smiled happily as he held out one of the sticky ice cream cones to Lizzie and the other to Ellynne. Lizzie took hers and licked it quickly, squealing with delight, "Ooh, Banana Nut. My favorite."

Bruce ate the ice cream cone that Ellynne refused. "These were for a couple of girls I met here but they were melting. You lucked out."

Lizzie smiled at Bruce and if Ellynne didn't know better she would have said that Lizzie was flirting. "Lucked out. We sure did. Imagine meeting you here. It's just wonderful."

Standing there in the sun watching Lizzie smile at Bruce and Bruce smile at Lizzie, Ellynne felt like the grump who stole Easter vacation. They were obviously enjoying themselves. Why shouldn't she? She said, "You have something in common. You both have such bright teeth they flash in the sunlight."

Bruce said to Lizzie, "Of course I would have met you Friday. You are coming to my beach party at home."

"I am?"

Ellynne frowned and gulped. She hadn't mentioned it to Lizzie. It was clear she would have to go to the beach party now.

Lizzie and Bruce walked slightly ahead, talking and laughing as though they were old friends. Ellynne was amazed to see how cheerful Bruce seemed to be with Lizzie. For the life of her, she couldn't see why he was so attracted to her. Though Lizzie didn't look as frumpy in her bikini as she did in her clothes, she still was a long way from the prettiest girl on the beach. There was nothing special about Lizzie's looks.

Bruce thought Lizzie was special though — that was clear. By the time they got to the little spot on the pebbled beach where Bruce had his towel, he was deep in the middle of a story about his last trip to New York City. Lizzie clutched her beach bag, held her straw hat against the sea breeze, and said, "Ooh! . . . Isn't that wonderful? . . . Imagine that . . . really? . . ." at appropriate moments.

It wasn't just Bruce who seemed to think Lizzie was special. When he and Lizzie walked along the water's edge, looking for one of the glass-bottomed boats that took people out sight-seeing, Charles and Arnold started quizzing Ellynne about her friend.

"Lizzie is an old friend from Ohio. She's here for the week," Ellynne said cautiously.

"She's nice," Charles said.

"Pretty too," Arnold added. Then he added, "Not a knockout like you, Ellynne, but pretty."

"She's an old friend," Ellynne mumbled and opened the book she'd brought. She couldn't decide whether to be happy that Lizzie was making such a hit or worried about what was going to happen when they got back to the mainland. Clearly, being away from Redondo Beach made everyone easier to please. She thought she knew enough about Bruce and Charlie and Arnold to know they wouldn't have looked twice at Lizzie if she were going to high school with them.

"The new girl always makes a splash," Lizzie said happily as she stepped out of the shower and towel-dried her close-cropped haircut. "I think it's just wonderful."

"I like your hair," Ellynne said. "I don't think I told you."

Lizzie looked at her and smiled softly, "No, I don't think you did."

Ellynne wondered if she detected a touch of sarcasm or at least a touch of criticism behind the soft reply. She didn't know quite what to say so she skirted the subject. "What time is Bruce picking us up?"

"He's out there right now," Lizzie said. "I heard his bike wheels." She slipped on a striped tee shirt and some faded Levis.

Ellynne looked at her friend in dismay. She asked, "Aren't you going to wear your shorts? The cute white ones?"

"No," Lizzie said practically. "My legs will get cut on the brush if I fall. Levis are all right."

Ellynne said nothing more. She was sure Bruce would lose interest in Lizzie now that he was about to see her at her most casual. Lizzie had never had much interest in clothes and she usually managed to buy things at least one size too big.

Bruce didn't lose interest though. He helped Lizzie on her bicycle as though she were the most precious person in the world. Ellynne had to help herself.

Ellynne felt a bit like a third wheel on the trip to the bird sanctuary. As Lizzie and Bruce talked with each other, laughing and joking and making plans for the rest of the vacation, Ellynne slipped into her own private dream world. What a different trip this would be if Kip Russell were beside her.

She wondered what Kip was doing this very moment, and then she smiled wryly at the question. Kip was working at the supermarket right this very moment. He was working full-time this week as a replacement for the assistant manager who was taking part of his vacation. It was a break for Kip, who would put all the extra money away for his college education.

Just thinking about Kip made Ellynne feel happier. She pedaled up the hill to the bird sanctuary, enjoying the cool breeze, the warm sunny air, and the sharp, sweet sounds of the birds. She invented another one of those long, romantic conversations between Kip and her dream-self. The best thing about daydreaming was that you always knew the right things to say. If the plot didn't seem to be working out exactly right, you could go back and start again.

Sometimes, Ellynne went as far as getting married to Kip when they were both in college. Usually, she got as far as the engagement party and started backwards. Even in her dreams, Ellynne wasn't sure she was ready to make such a permanent commitment. What she was sure of was that she wanted to be asked!

Ellynne pedaled along behind Lizzie and Bruce, listening to them. Why couldn't she and Kip ever seem to just enjoy each other the way these two seemed to? It seemed to Ellynne that instead of growing closer together, she and Kip had come to a certain spot in their romance and stopped. They still saw each other every week or two. They still enjoyed many of the same things. Ellynne sometimes wondered if Kip would be asking her out at all if it weren't for their mutual interest in old music. Though she still loved kissing Kip good-night, he always seemed on his guard around her. It was almost as though he didn't want to get any closer to her than he already was.

Life hurts, Ellynne decided sadly and went back to her dream. This time, she started with the point where she won the cheerleading spot and Kip came up to her after the contest, holding open his arms. "My darling," he murmured as his arms wrapped around her fiercely . . .

"Ellynne! Ellynne! Wake up!" Lizzie was half-laughing, half-yelling.

There was a large tree root directly in front of her path. Ellynne swerved her bike, it bounced, and she slid to the ground. Her first thought was, *I've hurt my leg.* Her second thought was, *I'll lose the contest.*

Lizzie and Bruce bent over her with concern. Lizzie said, "It's just a sidewalk burn. Remember them? We used to get them all the time when we were kids."

Ellynne looked down at her skinned knees and smiled ruefully. "I'll look really glamorous when I try out for cheerleader with these skinned knees."

Bruce and Lizzie helped her up. Lizzie said, "I'll bet you were daydreaming again."

Ellynne blushed as Lizzie confided to Bruce, "When we were in the seventh grade, Ellynne used to make up these marvelously romantic stories. I thought she had real talent. In fact, she's still my favorite author. Do you remember the one about the White Prince, Ellynne?"

Ellynne wished fiercely that the earth would swallow her up. *Better yet, she wished the earth would swallow Lizzie!* It wasn't bad enough that she was going to have to go to the cheerleading contest with skinned knees, but now Lizzie was entertaining Bruce with blow-by-blow accounts of what she and Ellynne were like in seventh grade.

After they'd washed off the skinned knees, plastered them with iodine, and were sitting in the coffee shop of the bird sanctuary, Lizzie was still rattling on. Bruce obviously thought Lizzie was charming, but Ellynne reflected gloomily that he would have an entirely different image of her by now.

As Lizzie launched into the story of how she and Ellynne had won their Girl Scout medals in bird watching, Ellynne interrupted, "Lizzie, I feel a little like you're my mother showing pictures of me on a bearskin rug. Could we change the subject?"

Lizzie stopped suddenly, looked hurt, then said quietly, "Sure, Ellynne. I just forgot."

Bruce put his hand over Lizzie's protectively and said, "I love your stories, and I'll bet you were the best bird watcher in Dayton."

"Not really," Lizzie said. "There was a girl named SueLou Murphy — that was her real name — SueLou — who got all the badges first. SueLou's father had been a scoutmaster for all six of her older brothers, and she felt she had to be better than any of them to compete. At least that's what we told ourselves back in the seventh grade. We were amateur psychologists that year." She turned to Ellynne and asked, "Do you remember when we checked out all of Sigmund Freud's works?"

Realizing she was beaten, Ellynne laughed and said, "Sure, I remember. We didn't understand a word of them but we thought we were very smart."

They spent the rest of the afternoon and evening with Bruce. That evening, Bruce took them dancing at the casino, and though he was obviously more interested in Lizzie than Ellynne, he was careful to dance with them both.

At midnight, they said good-bye to Bruce who would be taking the first plane home the next morning. His last words were, "Don't forget. Day after tomorrow is mine. And the beach party is Thursday."

Lizzie's eyes were shining as she promised, "I won't forget. I think it's just wonderful that you're being so nice to me."

Ellynne cringed at her friend's unsophisticated enthusiasm for Bruce Davidson. Hadn't
Lizzie ever heard of playing hard to get?
Didn't she know anything about appearing
aloof and desirable? Though she had to
admit that Lizzie seemed to be holding Bruce
Davidson's interest this evening, she dreaded
the next encounter. Surely, he would see that
Lizzie was just a young, unsophisticated
child compared to attractive girls like Merri
and Willie and, yes, herself.

*Am I jealous because Bruce prefers Lizzie
to me?* Ellynne asked herself. The answer
was only a faint yes. She wasn't the least bit
interested in Bruce. She was only interested
in Kip. No. She wasn't jealous. She was glad
that Lizzie was having such a good time. She
was only nervous about what was going to
happen next.

Eighteen

What happened next was that Lizzie and Bruce spent the next two days together. Ellynne found that she needn't have worried about entertaining Lizzie at all.

When they got off the plane at the harbor in Wilmington, Bruce was waiting for them. He said, "I called your mother and told her I'd pick you up. She said it was O.K."

That afternoon, he took Lizzie to a play in Hollywood. The next day, he took her to visit Universal Studios where his father worked. Lizzie went everywhere in her one "good" dress she'd brought. Privately, Ellynne thought the print was too old and dull for a teenager, but she had to admit that Lizzie looked as though she was glowing with happiness as she wore it.

That evening, she confided to Ellynne, "Bruce says I have lovely skin and hair." She ran her hand over her close-cropped curls. "He says he'd like to see it longer. What do you think, Ellynne? Shall I let it grow?"

"I like it better short," Ellynne said. "Besides," she teased, "you're only going to be here three more days. It won't grow much in three days." Ellynne was feeling relaxed and happy. It was wonderful to see her old friend having such a wonderful time. It was also nice not to feel she had to entertain her all the time.

Lizzie's face dimpled and she fairly burst with the news. "Guess what? Bruce's father will be working in Chicago this summer. Bruce will be coming to see me in Dayton."

"That's great. Keep your hair cut close," Ellynne said. "It's more sophisticated."

Lizzie looked critically in the mirror. "I don't know. Bruce says he doesn't like sophisticated women. He's had two stepmothers and they were both sophisticated. Bruce says he thinks women should be natural."

Ellynne nodded. "I'm glad Bruce can see what a wonderful person you are, Lizzie."

Impulsively, Lizzie threw her arms around Ellynne and hugged her tight. "Isn't it wonderful! Isn't everything wonderful! Oh, thank you. Thank you."

Even though things were going so well, Ellynne couldn't help being nervous about Bruce's party the next day. After all, Bruce might think Lizzie was fine, but Bruce was something of an outsider himself. He certainly wasn't one of the most popular kids in the school.

Those kids were at the party though. There were about twenty seniors and juniors playing volleyball by the time Lizzie and Ellynne got there. Lizzie looked at Ellynne reproachfully and said, "See, I told you we'd be late."

Ellynne whispered, "But you look great." They'd spent the morning buying Lizzie a bikini that Ellynne thought looked impressive enough.

"I feel naked," Lizzie grumbled. But she seemed to enjoy the attention she got from the two fellows she'd met in Catalina. When Bruce came out of his house and put his arm around her, asking her to come help him put the rest of the refreshments on the table, she beamed with joy.

Ellynne looked around for Kip and her heart sank when she saw that he was talking with Merri. When Merri insisted on rubbing tanning lotion on his back, Ellynne couldn't stand it. She ran past the volleyball players, down the wide beach to the water.

She dove into the waves, swimming directly out to sea. Her hair would be a mess but she didn't care. She didn't care about anything but getting rid of the awful, hurt, and lonely feeling that she carried around inside her these days. Kip hadn't called her once this week, and she'd missed him. Surely he knew that? Maybe he didn't care about her at all.

The months of exercising to get ready for

the cheerleading really paid off in the water, Ellynne noticed. She was amazed to discover that she'd swum past the breakwater without even feeling winded. *Even if I don't win*, Ellynne thought, *I'm in better shape than I've ever been in my life*.

She swam until she was exhausted, then she floated for a while before she turned to come back to shore. The trip back to the beach seemed longer and much harder than it had on the way. By the time she could touch bottom, she was moving slowly, with difficulty.

Ellynne walked past the volleyball players without speaking, dropped onto her towel, and fell fast asleep. When she woke, the sun was slanting low and she shivered in the late afternoon breeze.

Kip asked, "Ellynne, are you all right?"

Ellynne sat up, crossed her feet, and hugged her knees. "I was dreaming," she said slowly. "In my dream, I was floating away on a cloud. It was beautiful."

Kip laughed. "You look a little like Ophelia with the bedraggled locks, a little like the golden princess in a fairy tale."

Ellynne put one hand on her hair. It was dry and it must look awful. With long, straight hair like hers, she should have showered immediately and brushed it out. Now it would look like damp, tangled seaweed all evening. Maybe she could find a scarf.

"Aren't you going to eat?" Kip asked. "Nearly everyone else is on the deck right now. The hot dogs are almost gone."

"How long have I been asleep?" she asked.

"I don't know," Kip admitted. "But judging from the sunburn on your back, I'd say it has been a while." He reached out and touched her shoulder.

As always, when Kip touched her, Ellynne wanted to lean closer to him, to have him hold her in his arms. She laughed lightly and moved away from him, saying, "I took a very ambitious swim, too ambitious, I guess."

"You all right?" Kip asked.

"Certainly," Ellynne answered. She knew her voice sounded unnatural. How could she tell him how she was really feeling? How could she tell him how it hurt her to see him with Merri?

Kip took her hand and said, "Let's go eat. Your friend is nice. Funny, I got the idea that you didn't really think I'd like her. I wasn't going to call you until she left. But I do like her. She's nice. Funny too."

Funny? All of Ellynne's nervousness returned. She wondered what sort of funny stories Lizzie was telling now. When they got up on the deck, she hadn't put the mustard on her hot dog before her worst fears were confirmed.

Merri waved to them and shouted, "Over here, Kip. Lizzie's telling this delightful story about Ellynne's first love affair. Come on, you'll just scream."

Ellynne held her plate with shaking hands and followed Kip over to a group of kids who were toasting marshmallows on a portable grill. Merri looked up at Ellynne and said maliciously, "Your friend, Lizzie, has just been telling us the funniest things about you."

Ellynne sat down on a stool slightly to the outside of the group. She went absolutely numb as she heard Merri say to Lizzie, "Go on, tell us what she did next."

Lizzie laughed and said, "Well, we wrote to Paul Pearson, of course. And he answered. See, that's what makes it all so funny. Here we were, two little seventh graders and this guy answered our letter. How were we to know he wanted to make his girlfriend jealous. Anyway, Ellynne wrote these wonderful letters to him and sometimes I helped. I remember, I wrote, 'Your eyes are pools of passion.' Do you remember that, Ellie?"

Lizzie turned to Ellynne and waited for a reply. Ellynne said nothing but Merri didn't really give her a chance. Merri urged Lizzie on. "And what happened next? Did she ever go out with him?"

Lizzie looked shocked. "Why no. We were only in the seventh grade and he was a senior."

"Let's see," Merri said, "in the seventh grade you must have been about ten, weren't you, Ellie?"

Ellynne's paper plate crumpled in her clutched fingers. The mustard from her hot dog ran onto her leg. She said stiffly, "Eleven, I was eleven."

"No you weren't," Lizzie corrected. "At least not at the beginning. I remember I was eleven and you were even younger. In fact, that's the way we became friends in the first place. We were the youngest in the class."

"Isn't that cute," Merri said. Her voice was just dripping with sarcasm, but Lizzie couldn't apparently hear it. Ellynne wondered if Lizzie was unable to recognize malice because she never felt it. Was Lizzie really that good a person?

"Do tell us about her first date," Merri urged.

"Why Ellynne never dated in Ohio," Lizzie blurted out innocently. "Her first date was with Kip."

Merri shrieked with laughter. The other kids took up the cue and laughed along with her. Lizzie looked from one teen to the other and suddenly realized that she had said something wrong. Mutely, she turned to Ellynne to ask for forgiveness.

Ellynne looked away from Lizzie's stricken face to the paper plate on her lap. The laughter of Merri and her friends seemed to grow louder and louder. Between gasps, Merri asked, "Is that really true? Kip was her first date?"

Kip's voice cut acoss the laughter with

scorn. He said, "Merri, Lizzie doesn't lie. She's telling the truth, though why you think it's so funny is beyond me. I think it's nice."

He leaned toward Ellynne to hug her, but she had already leaned toward Lizzie, whose face was crumpling into tears. Ellynne patted Lizzie on the shoulder protectively as she said, "Lizzie is telling the truth. I was in love with Paul for months, and then he joined the army and broke my heart. After that, I read a lot of books and played it safe." She smiled at Lizzie and said gently, "Isn't that right?"

Lizzie looked up gratefully at her friend and shook her head in agreement. "We talked a lot about boys," she said, "but neither of us ever dated."

Again, Merri laughed. "Isn't that darling!" she said. "Just darling." She looked around the group, waiting for them to join her in the derision, but before the others could take the cue, Kip's voice cut across the first hesitant peals of laughter.

"Shut up," he said.

Ellynne wanted to kiss him right there in front of everyone. All of a sudden, she didn't really care what Merri and her friends thought of her as long as Lizzie wasn't hurt.

She realized that she had been selfish and thoughtless when she had worried about what the others would think about Lizzie. Lizzie was a much more important person to her than Merri Merriweather. What anyone thought of Lizzie didn't matter anymore.

Merri realized that she'd made a big mistake by openly ridiculing Lizzie and Ellynne and tried to make up for it by being nice to Lizzie after that.

Once, she said, "How would you and Ellynne like to come to my house tomorrow? You could use the pool and Ellynne and I could practice for the contest."

Lizzie shook her head, "No, thanks. I'm going to Disneyland with Bruce and Ellynne."

"Maybe I can come too?" Kip asked Ellynne directly.

Ellynne shook her head, yes, a warm feeling in her heart as she realized that Kip had asked her out in front of everyone. Apparently, he was through worrying about hurting Merri's feelings.

Nineteen

Disneyland was like a dream for Ellynne. It was one of those days in her life that seemed absolutely perfect in every respect. Bruce picked Lizzie and her up at ten, and then they all picked up Kip at ten-fifteen. By eleven, they were walking across the bridge into the Magic Kingdom.

Lizzie was like a small child as she squealed and jumped up and down, running from one glorious experience to another. For once, Lizzie's enthusiasm seemed to make the day even more perfect, and Ellynne was grateful for her friend's fun-loving nature.

Bruce was obviously enthralled by Lizzie's coltish joy at finding Disneyland exactly as she'd expected. At lunch, he said shyly, "You know, I've been here lots of times. When I was a kid, my stepmothers were always taking me here, and this is the first time I've truly enjoyed it."

Lizzie nodded sagely and said, "The best time to be a kid is when you're older. I'm never going to grow up."

Bruce took Lizzie's hand and pulled her toward the Matterhorn, asking, "Is that a promise?"

"A promise," Lizzie said gaily.

Ellynne and Kip stayed on the ground, choosing to sit on a park bench and watch the people go by. They were quiet most of the time, but once, Kip asked softly, "What would you think if I decided to stay at home next year?"

"Not go to college?" Ellynne asked.

"I'd go to El Camino Junior College one year. Actually, I'd go this summer, one year, and next summer. With that many credits, I could transfer to Berkeley as a junior when you graduate from high school. Or would you prefer Santa Cruz?"

"For me or you?" Ellynne asked.

"For us," he answered quickly.

"I'd prefer Berkeley," Ellynne said. "But if you want Santa Cruz . . ."

"Berkeley's fine," Kip said. He covered his hand with hers and said, "Your friend Lizzie is good for people."

"How do you mean?" Ellynne asked.

"She's good for Bruce because she makes him happy. He seems a lot less like a little old man these days. She's good for you because she makes you less . . . less self-conscious, I guess, and she's good for me because she made me see exactly what and who I care about."

Kip took her face in his hands and bent over her as he whispered, "It's you I care about, Ellynne. It has been you for a long time, but I guess I didn't know it or I didn't want to admit it."

Ellynne slipped her arms around his shoulders and drew him closer. "It doesn't matter why. The important thing is that you feel that way."

They kissed warmly, softly, and completely, and then they sat in happy silence on the bench waiting for Lizzie and Bruce to return.

When Lizzie and Bruce came down from the Matterhorn, they all went to Tom Sawyer's Island together. Then they circled back to the Jungle Ride and later skipped over to the Haunted House. On just about every ride, Bruce had an anecdote about his childhood. Most of the stories were tragi-comic.

On the Jungle Ride he said, "This is where my first stepmother got my father to propose. I remember it was raining that day and we were riding around in the river while it rained on us. I can remember thinking that the river might fill up so high that we'd drown. Funny how worried I was when I was a kid. I don't worry much anymore."

Ellynne and Lizzie and Kip all giggled, but none of them told Bruce he was considered quite a worrier by the other kids. They didn't want to worry him.

After Tom Sawyer's Island, there was the band concert, the trips through the shops, the visits to the exhibits. After dark, they danced a while in one of the outdoor discos and then they ate hot fried crullers and chocolate at the French Pavilion.

On the way home, Ellynne sighed and said, "I'm stuffed. I'm tired. I'm sleepy and I wish this day would never end."

"So do I," Lizzie wailed. "Do you realize I have to go home tomorrow night?"

"Why not stay an extra week?" Bruce suggested. His voice wasn't quite as casual as his words.

"You don't know my folks," Lizzie moaned. "They'd think I suggested dropping out of school permanently if I suggested such a thing."

"Call them," Ellynne urged. "Tell them I need moral support. Tell them I'm trying out for cheerleader on Monday and I'll need you to pick up the pieces or help me celebrate." She smiled to herself. A week ago, having Lizzie at the tryouts would have seemed like the worst thing that could have happened. Now it seemed like a good idea. She'd grown up a bit in these last few days.

"Wouldn't that be wonderful," Lizzie said. "And I could meet Willie. Are you sure . . .?" Lizzie asked shyly. "I wouldn't want to cramp your style, Ellie."

Ellynne smiled at her oldest friend and said with complete honesty, "I'd love to have you there. In victory or defeat, we're buddies."

Lizzie nodded. "They won't let me stay a week," she said. "But they probably will let me stay an extra two days. Your mother wouldn't mind driving me to the airport on Tuesday night instead of tomorrow?"

"I'll drive you," Bruce said. "An extra two days isn't an extra week but it's better than nothing. I'll take you to Marineland tomorrow, and Monday we'll drive down the coast for lunch. You haven't seen any of the beach towns."

"Wait a minute," Lizzie laughed. "I'm supposed to be staying to give Ellynne moral support."

"The contest is after school. I'll bring you back for that," Bruce promised. Then his brow crinkled in worry. "Maybe it would be better to drive down the coast tomorrow and go to Marineland on Monday."

"Don't worry about me," Ellynne said sleepily as she leaned her head against Kip's shoulder. "I'll be practicing all day tomorrow. So you can have fun and show up at the school cafeteria at two-thirty on Monday."

"Are you sure?' Lizzie asked. "I don't want to do anything to upset you. I know how much you want to win. I know that being a cheerleader is very important to you."

"Yes, it is important," Ellynne agreed. "And I'd like you to be there. Win or lose."

"Don't even think of losing," Lizzie chided. "You're going to win."

Am I? Ellynne wondered. *Could it be that that dream will also come tru*e?

Twenty

Willie and Lizzie were instant friends. Ellynne watched amusedly as they bustled around her, fixing her short costume, brushing her hair, applying last-minute spots of rouge, and insisting that she not be nervous. "*You're* both so nervous you act as though I were getting married."

"*Anyone* can get married," Willie said scornfully.

"Bend over," Lizzie said. "I want to make sure your shorts aren't too tight for the stretches."

Merri came into the dressing room, looked around for a spot to change, and when she saw them said, "Hi. Aren't you nervous? I'm just so nervous I could die."

"You'll make it," Willie said shortly.

A stab of fear shot through Ellynne. *What am I doing in this contest?* she thought. Even after months of work, she knew she wasn't as good as Willie or Merri. They were both naturals who bent, jumped, and twisted with the ease of cats. Willie's style was longer, leaner, more languid than Merri's, but they were both good. *There are two vacant places,* Ellynne reminded herself.

At the same time, Willie said aloud, "There are two spots. You'll get one, honeychile."

"There are six other girls. They're all good," Ellynne reminded her. Somehow, she thought Willie was going to be very disappointed if she didn't make the team. Funny to think that she would be trying to prepare Willie for the loss. *I guess I've done some growing,* Ellynne thought. Of course she wanted to win; she wanted to win very, very much. But either way she would be all right. She took a deep breath and thought of Kip. If she closed her eyes, she could almost imagine that she was sitting beside Kip again.

A feeling of warmth spread over Ellynne as she remembered what Kip had said to her yesterday. *It's you I care about, Ellynne.* How sweet those words had been to hear.

"Stop dreaming," Willie chided. "You look silly with that dreamy smile on your face. You're supposed to be nervous."

Ellynne laughed. "I'm nervous. Believe me, I'm nervous. Oh, Willie, I do want to win!" She hugged her friend and whispered, "Thanks for helping me . . . either way. . . ."

"You're better than they are," Willie growled. "Susie's too bouncy, Laura's too slow, and Marsha's too black."

From the very beginning, Willie had discounted Marsha as a possible competitor because she was black. "Honeychile, believe me. I know. They'll have one black chick on the team but never two. Two would be a majority. Heaven forbid."

The coach blew her whistle and all the chatter stopped. The cheerleader contestants went through the door without a sound. They had been warned that noisy voices or nervous laughter could turn off the judges.

Ellynne felt the muscles in her stomach tighten in fear. She felt a little light-headed as she scanned the large, almost empty gymnasium. Yes, there was Lizzie with a brave smile on her face. Too bad they wouldn't let any of the male students into the gym during the tryouts. It might have been easier if Kip had been out there smiling at her, sending her silent messages of love and encouragement.

She wasn't really listening to the coach's instructions. She'd heard them before. In practice, the coach had been careful to go over and over the actual routine for tryouts. Coach Barnes wanted to be sure that the girl with the best ability won. She'd tried to prepare them as well as she could for the inevitable nervousness. Now, as she talked, Ellynne was grateful for that preparation. At least she knew what was expected. That was a big help. Still, her knees were beginning to tremble. Whoever heard of a cheerleader with shaky knees?

The coach said, "Good luck," and bent to turn on the record player. There it was, the familiar beginning to the familiar march. Quickly, Ellynne dropped into line beside Marsha. One, two, three, kick. Turn to the left and kick higher. Higher!

The first portion of the tryout was really a warmup session. The girls performed together in a line. They marched, jumped, and kicked to music. This portion did two things, according to Coach Barnes. It gave the other judge a chance to look the girls over and separate them in her own mind. *All pretty girls look alike to adults*, the coach had said. Though the girls giggled at the thought, they knew she was probably right.

It also gave the girls a chance to warm up and get over their nervousness. As Ellynne ran through the familiar steps, she felt herself relax. *I'm good*, she thought. *I may not be the best but I'm really very good.*

Ellynne went through the standard cheers without a mistake. She kicked higher than she ever had in her life. Only Marsha kicked higher than she. She jumped almost as well as Merri and better than most of the other girls. As the line ended, Willie whispered, "You did well. I'm sure of that."

"Did you see Marsha?" Ellynne asked. "She's good."

"Yeah, but don't worry about Marsha. You'll make it, kid. You'll make it."

Now it was time for the teams of two to

work together. The girls were allowed to watch quietly. She would work with Marsha. Merri and Laura would work together. Willie's part in the tryouts was over. She had been in the line but Coach Barnes had said it was a farce to make her do the full tryout.

Willie left the girls and went to sit beside Lizzie on the bench. Each contestant had been able to invite one girl to watch. There were a few teachers who were also looking on. Ellynne watched Willie and Lizzie watching her. *It's an unfair advantage*, she thought. *I've got two rooters and the other girls only have one*. Again, she thought of Kip and she thought *Three. Kip is right outside that door and he's rooting for me too.*

Coach Barnes motioned to her. Now it was her turn. Her and Marsha's turn to show what they could do. They picked up the pompoms and bounced onto the center of the gym floor. Facing each other, they bowed and then reached high in the air, waving the bright strands of paper as they began.

> Turn it on
> Turn it on
> *(clap, clap)*
> Turn it on
> With power and might.
> Turn it on
> With spirit and fight.
> Redondo! Redondo!
> Fight. Fight. Fight.

Their portion of the tryouts lasted exactly two minutes. They moved gracefully, surely, and well. As they bounded off the center area, Ellynne felt she had done well. Whatever happened, she had done her best.

By four-fifteen, it was all over except the waiting. Coach Barnes looked at them and said, "Don't go far. We should have a decision within an hour."

Ellynne was grateful that Coach Barnes made it a practice to give the contestants a quick decision. She had heard that in most schools the girls had to wait two or three days. This way, the pain would be sharp and quick but it would be over. *Soon*, Ellynne promised herself. *Soon, there will be no more waiting.*

As she pulled on her clothes, Ellynne felt very calm. She wasn't quite sure why she felt this way. Maybe she was really terribly nervous and she had buried it. Maybe, but right now she was just happy that the contest was over. She knew she'd worked hard. She knew she'd done well.

As she brushed her hair, she remembered that Kip was waiting for her. He was either outside right now or he would be very soon. All she had to do was remember that Kip was on the other side of these walls and she felt warm and wonderful again.

Ellynne wondered if she dared slip out of the dressing room into the side yard. From there, she could go around to the front entrance of the gym where Kip would be waiting with other interested males who had been refused admittance. But no, she didn't dare. Coach Barnes would never forgive her if she caught her sneaking out to meet her boyfriend.

She picked up her sweater and walked out of the dressing room into the gym. Joining Lizzie and Willie on the bleachers, she felt all the old nervousness return. They wanted her to win so much. Well, she wanted to win too. Suddenly, the knots tightened in her stomach. She looked around at the other girls. *They all want to win,* she reminded herself.

Most of them looked younger and awkward now. Only Merri and Marsha looked calm. *Merri is sure she's won. Marsha's sure she's lost,* Ellynne thought. *But this is a contest. Nothing is sure.*

Ellynne saw Virginia Hanson sitting straight and tall. *She wanted this so much,* Ellynne thought. Suddenly, Ellynne felt very sorry for Virginia and all the other girls who wanted to be cheerleaders but never would be. For the first time, Ellynne understood why her mother was so sure having cheerleaders at a game wasn't a good idea at all.

Coach Barnes was speaking now. She introduced Lydia Langtree who beamed at the girls, smiling wide and smoothing the charm over the losers like balm over raw wounds.

"Such talented girls," she gushed. "We had such a hard time making up our our minds. Any one of you girls was good enough, and in the end, it was only a teeny-weeny bit of difference that made the winners. There are no losers, you understand. No girl who looks like you girls or acts like you girls or has such great talent as you girls could consider herself a loser."

The contestants shuffled and moved nervously as Ms. Langtree rattled her paper and peered over the edge of her dark glasses. "The winners are Merri Merriweather and Marsha Browning."

For a moment, there was stunned silence. No one, absolutely no one, including Marsha, had really expected Marsha to win. Ellynne was the first to rise and move forward to where Marsha was standing. She threw her arms around the short, black girl and said, "Congratulations, Marsha. You deserved it."

Willie was right behind her, saying, "Isn't it wonderful? I never thought they'd . . ." and then she burst into tears.

Marsha nodded and put her arm around Willie, saying, "It's all right. I know you wanted Ellynne. It's all right."

Ellynne watched as girls burst into tears all around her. Merri and Willie were crying more loudly than the losers.

Lizzie wailed, "It's just awful. You were the best, Ellie. You were the best."

Ellynne shook her head. "You know that isn't true. Marsha was better and the judges chose her. Now let's go get a Coke. It's all over."

Willie and Lizzie were still crying as they left the gym. Ellynne was too busy looking for Kip in the crowd of young men standing outside the door. Then, suddenly, he was there, putting his arm around her protectively as he asked, "Are you all right?"

Ellynne could only smile and lean her head against his shoulder. She was watching Lizzie sob loudly as she told Bruce of the decision. Willie and Lizzie seemed to be vying for the role of dramatic heroine in a tragic opera. They were both talking to Bruce at once.

"Let's get out of here," Ellynne said. "I'm getting embarrassed."

Kip hugged her tightly and asked again, "Are you all right?"

She nodded her head, looking up at Kip's warm smiling face. *How very lucky I am,* she thought. The realization that Kip Russell was beside her, caring for her, and really worrying about her hit her sharply. She felt, for a moment, just a little breathless.

Kip bent and kissed her lightly on the forehead as they walked into the soda shop.

Because it was late, there weren't many kids inside. Ellynne was glad of that because Willie and Lizzie were still crying as though their hearts would break. She leaned against

Kip's shoulder and smiled at her loyal friends. She wanted to say to them that it wasn't the end of the world. She would have liked to tell them that being a cheerleader was nice but not the most important thing in the world. But she knew they wouldn't really believe her. They would think she was putting on a brave face.

Between sobs, Lizzie jumped up and said, "I forgot. I've got to call your mother. I promised her I would."

"My mother? She's in school."

Lizzie nodded and blew her nose. "I'm supposed to call her the minute we hear." She crumpled into tears again.

Ellynne slid out of the booth and said, "I'll call. You're too upset."

Kip was standing beside her as she dialed the U.C.L.A. Law Library and asked timidly, "Is there any way I can talk to Judith Aleese?"

Kip's warm breath on her neck and ear made her want to lean back, to turn her head for a kiss. She smiled at him and moved away slightly as the librarian asked, "Is this Ellynne?"

Amazed, Ellynen answerd. "Yes. Ellynne Aleese. I'd like to speak to my mother, Judith Aleese."

"She's right here," the librarian said. "We've been waiting for your call."

Ellynne greeted her mother quickly. "I lost. Marsha won. I'm kind of proud of the judges for choosing her. She was the best but she was black so everyone sort of discounted her. We thought the judges would go for a racial balance that was the same as the school."

To her absolute amazement, Judith Aleese was close to tears. "Oh honey, I'm so sorry," she wailed.

"Mother," Ellynne reminded her. "You're in a law library."

"People cry in libraries," Judith sniffed. "When my daughter loses something she wants, I have a right to feel sorry." She sniffed and asked in a more normal voice, "How do you feel?"

Ellynne knew her mother would believe her. Her mother would understand that she could be sorry to lose a contest and feel fine at the same time. "I feel just wonderful," she answered. "I feel as though I'm one of the luckiest people in the world. I've got a wonderful mother, wonderful friends, wonderful health, a wonderful boyfriend . . ." She paused for a quick smile at Kip who was still standing close. "I've got a wonderful future and I know that next year will be the most wonderful one yet."

"You really mean that, don't you?" her mother asked.

"I really mean it," Ellynne said as she hung up the phone and turned to kiss Kip and go back to her friends.

204